ERIC GOEBELBECKER

CLOUDS IN THE FUTURE

THE GREAT WAR OF THE WORLDS BOOK #2

Trick of the Tale LLC

25 Veterans Plaza #5279

Bergenfield, NJ 07621-9998

For Dad

FOREWORD

The Great War of the Worlds stories are set in a universe where H.G. Wells's War of the Worlds happened.

In 1894, aliens crashed to Earth in spacecraft that operated like meteorites. They attacked us with fearsome weapons like Black Smoke, a chemical weapon and heat rays that can melt steel in a few seconds. Then, they built processing centers and used humans for food.

But the attack ended quickly because the Martians, if that was where they really came from, weren't prepared to deal with Earth's microbes and died from disease.

What happened after the attack? What did humanity do with the technology the Martians left behind?

"When, when?" I sighed.
The one I longed for
Has finally come;
With her now,
I have all that I need.

RYOKAN

PROLOGUE

MARCH 1915: WEGENER'S COMPOUND, NEAR REIMS, FRANCE

The retrofitted sniper scope on the M98 restricted Hauptmann Ritter's field of vision, but the blood spray when the round hit General Wegener in the chest was impossible to miss. Zimmerman hadn't made that shot. He was good, but not that good.

Ritter panned over and spotted the shooter: the tall, dark-haired sycophant with the trimmed mustache. Beckenbauer? Was that his name? He'd been an impressive sniper in training exercises.

Ritter glanced back at Wegener then. The general was lying on the parade field like a pile of soiled linens as Zimmerman and his fat Unteroffizier reached him. Why were they even bothering? Even though the shot hadn't been through Wegener's heart, he didn't have long.

The stupid bastard had asked for it anyway. Ritter had told Wegener that trusting Zimmerman was a mistake, and that he should avoid angering the Martians with his toy Panzer. But the fool had done both. All because he'd thought he could shoot his way out of trouble. That trick had only worked once.

Just then, Ritter noticed Zimmerman was kneeling over the

general's body. He seemed to be talking. Was Wegener still breathing?

Ritter trained the scope on Zimmerman's head. A gentle squeeze, and half of Wegener's mistakes would be gone.

But that would be suicide. Zimmerman and his men weren't soldiers, but they were decent enough fighting men. They'd figure out where the shot came from, and Beckenbauer was still holding that rifle.

The best revenge, Ritter had once been told, was living well. He disagreed. Now was the time for him to quietly exit the battlefield and live to fight again—and save his vengeance for later.

The Martians needed a new ally anyway. A real soldier. A man who knew how to get things done.

CHAPTER 1
AUGUST 1915: GOUSSAINVILLE, FRANCE

The little girl danced on the edge of the well, teetering and waving her arms to catch her balance. Christian Beckenbauer lunged forward with his hands outstretched, but pulled up short when the girl's father stepped in to catch her.

It was easy to understand the little girl's exuberance. Her tiny fingers clutched what was probably the first piece of bread she'd seen in a couple of weeks, since the last time Christian and the rest of the Marauders had visited with supplies from Paris. But seeing her that close to falling into the well brought back unwelcome memories.

The tiny village of Goussainville sat on the northeastern edge of the area surrounding Paris. It was an area the Martians had left unmolested since withdrawing a few months earlier, but not before destroying rail service and decimating crops. Food was still in short supply, and what was available had to be distributed by foot, truck, or horse-drawn cart.

"Herr Beckenbauer?"

Christian turned to find Louis, who was overseeing the handing out of food to the townspeople. He was younger than

Christian, probably only twenty-two or twenty-three, with clothes that hung off him like an understuffed scarecrow. Louis must have been eating better before the invasion. He'd inherited the village market from his father, who'd been killed by the invaders in April as they'd torn through the area. Now, Louis was the closest thing to a mayor Goussainville had.

"Yes, Louis?" Christian replied.

"What should we do with these Bibles?" Louis asked, pointing to a crate perched on the end of one of the supply carts.

Christian looked around before answering. The monseigneur, who was in charge of the village's church, was nowhere in sight.

"Set them aside for when it gets cold in a couple of months," Christian answered. "They'll make great fuel."

"Now, now, I'm sure Louis can find another use for the cardinal's *generous* gifts," Emil Zimmerman said as he appeared from behind the cart with a smile that didn't quite reach his eyes. "They're for everyone. Louis, why don't you speak to the monseigneur and see if he has a plan for distributing them? He's taking confession at the église."

Louis nodded and left.

Once Louis was out of earshot, Emil faced Christian. "We talked about this already. You need to keep your feelings about the church to yourself. We need their help with supplies." Emil was small, noticeably shorter than Christian's two meters, with thinning, dark hair. But what he lacked in stature, he made up for in gravitas and intensity.

"We're already keeping these villages safe and delivering food to them," Christian responded. "Why do we have to distribute the church's trash and kiss up to the cardinal's man, too? The monseigneur can cart his books out here and hand them out himself."

"The Martians killed Goussainville's priest, so he has plenty to do already," Emil said. "We need to work with him because that's part of the deal, and we don't want to make any more trouble for the Resistance. Things are tenuous enough as it is."

"They're tenuous because of the cardinal's attitude toward *us* and the Resistance."

"Yes, he's got a problem with Madame Curie. We don't want him to have a problem with—"

A deep hum cut Emil off. A hum that, to Christian, almost sounded like a Martian heat ray. But not quite.

The square exploded into pandemonium, with people running, screaming, and diving for cover wherever they could find it. Emil and Christian ran to the shelter of a nearby building.

"Martians?" Emil asked, scanning the horizon. "Where? I don't see any Wanderers."

"Is it me, or did that heat ray sound . . . wrong?" Christian asked.

Emil nodded. "No, it's not you. Wrong pitch."

The tone was too high, as if it was from a smaller weapon. Were the Martians deploying less sizable Wanderers? Or using a new weapon?

Christian craned his neck and listened. Shots rang out from the northern end of the village, followed by another hum.

Emil had posted men at the end of the town because that was where he expected any ravageur attack to come from. Were the guards wasting rounds on a Wanderer? They knew better than that.

During the deadly Martian Attack earlier that year, Emil had led the squad that formed the heart of the Marauders safely out of the trenches in the Somme Valley. They'd marched all the way to Reims, where they'd toppled a wannabe military dictator and defended the city from even greater Martian aggression. Then they'd earned their nickname by staging a series of hit-and-run attacks on the Martians as they made their way to Paris, where they'd heard the Resistance needed help. Emil was a natural, if sometimes reluctant, leader.

"No Wanderer in sight," Emil said, bringing Christian back to the present, "and the men are firing at something. Go see what's happening over there. I'll check the southern end of town to make sure they aren't trying to box the village in."

"Send the Panzer my way once you're sure," Christian said. The Marauders had their Martian-powered electric Panzer, outfitted with its own heat ray, with them on this trip.

"If it's ravageurs, we need a prisoner. I'll give you some time before I send Fluse. You're our best shot. See if you can capture one of them before they run." Emil took off to the south then.

Christian worked his way north, taking cover between the buildings that lined the tiny village's main road as he went. The label "ravageurs" suited the mysterious and anonymous attackers Emil had referred to. They'd appear, open fire on villages, pilfer supplies, and retreat, often within minutes. Other than an uncanny capability to get away unscathed, they demonstrated no strategy or underlying goal.

But Emil thought they had heat rays now? That was absurd.

Soon, the familiar scent of a wood fire filled the air, confirming Christian's suspicion: Someone was using a heat ray. But most of the structures in Goussainville were stone. So what was burning?

The road ended with a two-story brick building, where a few Marauders huddled for cover. Two watched the field beyond the edge of town through their rifle sights. Beyond them, flames had engulfed a barn.

"What's happening?" Christian asked the big farm boy Emil affectionately called Bumpkin. He was tall, blond, and from somewhere deep in Bayern, with an endearing, almost childish naivete.

Bumpkin pointed at the open field, his eyes wide with fear. Christian squinted for a better view through the smoke and spotted the strangest vehicle he'd ever seen.

Someone had done their best to outfit an automobile like a Panzer, but their best wasn't very good. They'd attached metal plates—obviously salvaged from scrap—to its sides as armor, with irregular gaps on the front and sides, presumably so the driver could see and a crew could aim weapons.

But what might have been hilariously inept under other circumstances wasn't funny at all. The makeshift battle wagon had a heat ray bolted to its roof.

"We were over by the barn when that thing came out of the woods," Bumpkin said, his voice quavering. "It got Frenz."

Before Christian could reply, the heat ray fired on the bakery across the road. The building had been constructed from rough-cast walls but had wood-framed windows that immediately burst into flame.

Christian's jaw dropped as a woman fled out the front door. The vehicle turned its heat ray on her. She dropped to the ground screaming, then was incinerated in seconds.

The ray might have had a higher pitch, but it was at least as deadly as any on a Wanderer.

"We have to stop that thing before it kills everyone in Goussainville," said Miller, the metropolitan answer to Bumpkin. Tall, blond, and muscular, he had a fastidiously clean uniform and an imperious attitude.

"We need Fluse," Christian said. "But I don't know how much that thing will do before he makes it here."

"Can you shoot the mirror?" Miller asked. "Just like Zimmerman did? I can't make a shot like that, but I know you can."

Of course! That was how Emil had disabled the heat ray that had been accidentally triggered at the salvage yard. One well-placed shot, and this makeshift Panzer would be nothing more than a slow-moving automobile.

Christian eased himself into a prone firing position and brought his rifle sight up to his eye. He sighted the mirror and prepared to fire. Before he squeezed the trigger, the heat ray fired again, forcing him to look away.

A second person had exited the bakery and was engulfed in flames on the street.

Bile rose in Christian's throat. He sighted the crack in the armor and exhaled.

Then he squeezed the trigger. Pulled the bolt to eject the shell. Pushed it back to chamber the next round.

Aimed. Exhaled. Squeezed. Pulled. Pushed.

One more for good measure. Christian hoped with every fiber of his being that the murderers in the vehicle were dead.

So much for Emil's prisoners. These butchers were using Martian tech on civilians and belonged in Hell.

Finally, he targeted the mirror and shattered it with his fourth shot.

"What did you do that for?" Miller asked.

Christian turned to him and raised an eyebrow. "They friends of yours or something?"

"No! But we need to interrogate them. Find out where they got that thing."

"Next time you make the shot," Christian said, standing up.

The Marauders' Panzer rumbled up the road then, rolling over to where the three men were waiting. The huge steel vehicle spun on its tracks to face away from the enemy car, and Leutnant Fluse stepped out the back.

If the Marauders were a proper German unit, Fluse would have been their commander. Of course, if they were still German military, they'd be back in Germany instead of delivering supplies from Paris to the surrounding French villages.

Christian remembered how Fluse and Emil had been at each other's throats back at the Somme and struggled for control of the group all the way to Reims. Fluse, like his close friend Miller, looked and acted like the kaiser's ideal soldier. Emil had been, in many ways, the complete opposite. But they'd worked things out at some point during the struggle with Wegener, and now Emil was in charge.

"I think it's disabled," Christian said. "But lead us over there, and we can make sure."

Fluse reentered the Panzer, closing the door behind him. Christian fell in behind the vehicle with Miller, and they followed it to the automobile, using the Panzer as cover in a drill they'd practiced many times before.

"Great job, Beckenbauer," Miller growled once they opened the vehicle's doors. "They're dead!"

"No prisoner?" Emil said with a sigh as they met him back in the village.

Christian shook his head and explained what had happened.

"Why didn't you just shoot the mirror out?" Emil said, his head tilted.

"They were butchers!" Christian spat out.

"Butchers who could have told us where they got those weapons," Emil said.

The monseigneur stood behind Emil with his arms crossed, shaking his head. He was a heavyset man in his late twenties who, even though he was a man of the cloth, was particular about his grooming. His clean-shaven cheeks gleamed in the midday sun.

Heat rose in Christian's face, and a bead of sweat trickled onto his nose. "They had to be stopped. Who knows what they would have done if—"

"These weapons are our only advantage," Emil said, cutting him off. "And now someone else has them, too. We need to know more. Try to control your temper next time." He grimaced before adding, "We need to get more men trained so we can start creating garrisons. And we need Grundig to build us more weapons."

"I think you would have to talk to the cardinal before you start deploying an army around here," said the monseigneur in heavily accented German.

"Is he interested in protecting these people?" snapped Christian. "Or trying to restore the Holy Roman Empire? The cardinal isn't in charge of troop movements."

"Maybe if he was, you would know who these ravageurs were and what they wanted!" the monseigneur exclaimed.

"That's enough," Emil said. "Let's get back to Paris before sunset."

CHAPTER 2

THE MARAUDERS' HEADQUARTERS, PARIS, FRANCE

Christian steered the cart into the courtyard of the abandoned factory that served as the Marauders' headquarters. He guided the horses toward one corner and hopped off while a pair of local teens—brother and sister, if memory served—unhooked the horses and led them to water. The factory was less than a decade old and in wonderful condition, with solid brick walls and refined woodwork.

The complex made a nearly perfect headquarters for the group, with ample room for a training area, supply depot, and barracks. Like most of the factories on either side of the Seine, it was wired to the public power grid and outfitted with lights, heat, and an impressive array of electric equipment.

Paris had been devastated during the first Martian Attack fifteen years earlier, with more than twenty of the aliens' pods raining down inside the city limits. The Martians had set up their harvesting machinery right on the banks of the Seine. Most of the people who hadn't fled were killed, and many of the buildings not already destroyed by the falling spacecraft were damaged or destroyed.

After the first Martian Attack ended, the city rebuilt itself into an industrial powerhouse, with municipal electricity, government-subsidized housing for workers, and a completely revamped rail hub for distribution.

"Germany and the Americans used the alien technology to fight a war in Mexico, while France used it to help feed their people," Emil had quipped when they'd found the empty furniture factory.

The second Martian Attack earlier that year had hit the city harder than the first. Most people, including the government, had fled, while the workers left behind were turning to gangs for food and protection.

Still, this factory in Paris was the ideal location for the Marauders, especially for their research and development center run by Hauptmann Grundig, the man responsible for the weapon that had defeated the Martians at Reims. He'd also designed the heavily modified Panzer that Leutnant Fluse piloted, as well as an assortment of useful tools created from scavenged Martian technology. Grundig had been one of Wegener's most valuable officers, but his allegiance had proven flexible after they had toppled the erstwhile military ruler.

The Panzer, one of only a handful of A9Vs built for the kaiser's army, was already parked in the courtyard. Fluse had pulled ahead of Christian and the small convoy once they'd entered the city, most likely so he could get a head start on periodic maintenance.

The armored vehicle boasted dual electric motors and a turret-mounted heat ray, both fed by a Martian power supply. But despite having no massive diesel engine, the Panzer needed constant upkeep. Fluse was already replacing part of a track, while a young recruit from the Resistance swept the interior. The Marauders might have been a ragtag resistance group, but Leutnant Fluse still thought like a German officer.

The armored car, drawn by horses, pulled in behind Christian's cart. Even though the vehicle had been low on gasoline, Emil had deemed getting it away from Goussainville more important than recovering all their carts. So they'd hitched up a pair of horses and left one of their carts behind.

Christian had seen people incinerated by Martian heat rays before. It had happened when the aliens had attacked on the Somme, and again during the Battle of Reims. He'd also seen the German Army deploy its version of Black Smoke against Belgian troops.

But what he'd seen today in Goussainville was different. The heat rays had fired at bystanders. Innocent townspeople who were trying to escape. The ravageurs had to pay.

Every single one of them.

Christian opened the door to the main meeting hall and collided with Emil, who had ridden in the Panzer. The Marauders' leader might have been at least a head shorter than Christian, but he moved like a tractor. Christian stumbled back, extending his arms to regain his balance.

"Sorry! I need to run to the station. Berlin is online!" Emil said between gasps as he pushed past and jogged to the stables, presumably to grab a horse.

Christian knew the "station" was the Paris node in the Planetary Warning System, a global radio network built after the first Martian Attack. It had just come back online when the Marauders had arrived, but only with communications to the Anglische and Amerikaner nodes.

Since then, they'd learned that the second Martian Attack hadn't expanded to either England or the United States. At least not yet. But the Americans had suffered from internal strife that they weren't willing to talk about, while the Anglische were hunkered down, bracing for the aliens to reach their shores. Emil had shared the plans for Grundig's radioflash weapon with both countries, and they'd agreed to keep the lines of communication open.

And now there was a message from Berlin? The hairs on the back of Christian's neck stood up. There had been no word from home since the Martians had arrived on the Somme. The

Marauders had headed west after the Battle of Reims instead of back to Germany because they'd received word of the aliens moving on Paris.

Christian didn't have any family left in Germany. The Martians had incinerated their farm in Leimersheim during the first Attack, and he'd only survived because his grandfather had literally thrown him into a well. He'd treaded water for more than a day before he was finally found. Now he thought of the girl dancing on the edge of the well in Goussainville and shivered. Had the ravageurs killed her neighbor? Her mother? Or sister?

The monseigneur stepped into the hall, the aroma of the musky aftershave that followed him everywhere pulling Christian out of his reverie. "Where is Zimmerman?" the monseigneur asked.

"Hauptmann Zimmerman went to the station to pick up a message," Christian growled. "Is there something I can help you with?"

The first Martian Attack had created many German orphans like Christian. Most of them had been quietly shuffled off to orphanages run by the church, where, if they were lucky, the worst thing that happened to them was being used as cheap labor in a laundry.

Christian didn't like reminders of those days. And so he didn't like the monseigneur.

"I need to talk to him about the ravageurs, and his plans to garrison troops in the villages," the monseigneur said, bringing his eyes level with Christian's and putting his hands on his hips.

"We don't need to coordinate with the church," Christian said. Protecting people like the girl by the well was up to the Marauders, especially with the specter of ravageurs with Martian technology on the horizon. It wasn't up to the bloated fool in Notre-Dame or his fawning messenger.

"I don't think that's your decision," the monseigneur sneered.

"Then why are you wasting my time?" Christian turned to head toward the showers and his bunk. But not before he heard the monseigneur exhale loudly and stomp out of the hall.

Once Christian washed away the road dust and lingering perfume of gunpowder, he realized he was hungry. The Marauders' mess hall was the cafeteria, which had once been used to feed the factory's workers and still been equipped with long tables, benches, and a rudimentary kitchen when Christian and the others had found it. Hardly a day went by when he didn't marvel at their luck in finding the place.

Paris had been hit hard during the first Martian Attack, with more than twenty of the aliens' "meteors" falling within the city limits. So it was no surprise that Paris had cleared out quickly when word of the aliens' return spread. This factory, conveniently placed near the city center on the northern bank of the Seine, was about a decade old. It had likely been built as part of Paris's recovery after the first Attack.

Dinner was in full swing when Christian arrived at the mess hall. Roast rabbit, the first fresh squash of the season, and freshly baked raspberry tart. The Marauders ate well, better than most of the city's remaining residents, but they coordinated with the Resistance on a soup kitchen and pantry, too.

Hauptmann Grundig was seated alone at a table in one corner of the hall. Christian joined him, hoping to get an update on the armored car and see if he knew anything about the message from Berlin.

"Your trip north was rather eventful, Christian," Grundig said as Christian sat in the chair next to him. "You got another chance to show off your skill with that rifle." He smiled, his Smoke-stained teeth reminding Christian why the man usually ate alone.

"I'd rather be hunting boar than men," Christian said.

Grundig gave him another unsettling grin. "That didn't stop you from placing a few bullets inside the car."

"They deserved it. They used that heat ray on people who were only trying to run away. I wish I had my own heat ray so I could burn every one of them."

Grundig raised an eyebrow.

"What?" Christian said. "It's war, isn't it? An eye for an eye."

"A man named Christian, who hates the church, is quoting scripture," Grundig said, chuckling. It was a vaguely disturbing wheezing sound.

"Even a stopped clock is right twice a day."

"And what happens next?"

"What do you mean?"

"What happens when you run out of eyes?"

Christian sat in silence for a moment.

"Revenge makes for a cloudy future, Christian," Grundig went on. "We could have interrogated those men and found out where they got their rather *interesting* weapon. Taking revenge is an extremely bad trait." He held his hand up, as if addressing a larger audience.

"Another Bible quote?"

"Maimonides. An ancient scholar."

"I already got a lecture from Emil on not taking a prisoner."

"He's not wrong, is he?" Grundig asked. "The men are dead, and we know nothing about them or their weapons."

Christian crossed his arms and stared at his dinner plate.

"Anyway," Grundig continued, "I'm sure you saw how amateurish their armor was. It's a surprise it didn't fall off that Renault the first time they drove over a tree root. But that heat ray . . . Unglaublich! Whoever installed it has mastered concepts that took us months to figure out. Madame Curie has helped us make progress by leaps and bounds in the past few weeks. But whoever outfitted that car knows at least as much, if not more."

That sounded ominous to Christian. It meant the ravageurs

must have had more weapons to use on villagers. His mouth went dry at the thought of it, and he took a sip of coffee.

"Drinking coffee?" Grundig asked. "At this hour? That's not healthy. You should know better, Christian."

"Why? It's so weak it couldn't keep an infant awake. This swill's got more chicory than caffeine in it." Christian took another sip then. At least the coffee was warm.

"That stuff is bad for you. You should be more careful with what you put in your body."

Christian eyed Grundig's teeth and elected to change the subject. "Have you heard anything about this message from Berlin?" he asked.

"Not yet. Maybe they're recalling German soldiers."

Christian frowned.

"You don't want to go back, either?" Grundig asked.

Christian reeled back in his seat. What did Grundig mean by that?

"Oh, come now, Christian. You like it here as much as I do. You seem happier and more relaxed every day, although I'm not quite sure why. Me? I have everything I need here. A good lab with plenty of toys. A worthy intellectual partner in Madame Curie. It's even better than it was in Reims. What about you?"

The room fell away as Christian considered the question. Grundig was right. He *was* happy here. But why? Was decent food and a warm place to sleep all it took? Was it just that this was better than the trenches? Or was something else going on?

"Do I smell wood burning?" Emil said as he sat down at the other side of the table. "Or are you thinking?"

"You're back! You spoke to Berlin?" Grundig asked.

"Yes, I did. They got their Planetary Warning radios back on the air. All of Germany was down due to some kind of sabotage."

"Sabotage?" Christian repeated.

"Yes. Something with the systems in Eastern Europe and Russia knocked most of the network off the air. We didn't spend a lot of time talking about that." Emil paused to take a bite of rabbit. "What's really important is that they're recalling the troops."

"They want us home?" Christian asked.

"Ja. Frankfurt, Hamburg, and München were all hit pretty hard, along with the few troops the kaiser didn't already have deployed elsewhere. Based on what I heard, the Martians started in the east and have been working their way west. It sounds like Berlin is in the same position as Paris: just waiting for the other shoe to drop."

"But we're needed here!"

"We're needed there, too."

"But if the Martians are working their way west, they're coming here, too," Christian sputtered.

"We're part of the army," Emil responded. "Do we leave Berlin to the Martians and wait here?"

"What? You spent weeks denying you wanted anything to do with the army. You fought Fluse tooth and nail on that." By that point, Christian had raised his voice loud enough that people were looking up from their meals.

"Settle down," Emil said. "That was when the kaiser was trying to conquer Europe. Now I'm talking about protecting our home."

That made sense. Christian didn't want to hear it, but it made sense.

"They have supplies," Emil went on. "And for what might be the first time in history, our government is talking about a unified European defense force. Of course, the kaiser had to be presumed dead for that to happen, but I'll take it."

"Will they send us supplies to help defend Paris?" Christian asked.

"I'd hope so, but I think they may be more worried about home."

"But we came here to start a job. I want to finish it. And it's the German Army's fault that Paris is unprotected. Their soldiers were caught out in the trenches, fighting us when the Martians arrived." Christian crossed his arms then. This was what had happened in Reims. Things had gotten tough, and Emil had wanted to take off for home.

"That's an interesting take," Emil responded. "But we have a battalion of men here that belongs to Germany. Germany wants them back now, and the men might want to go home when they learn what's happening. Shouldn't they have a choice?" He shrugged.

"We *belong* to Germany?" Christian said.

"You know what I mean."

"I do, but I don't agree. And if they're really talking about a unified European force, then why can't we stay where we're needed? There are ravageurs out there, using heat rays on civilians. We need to find them and destroy them." Christian glanced at Grundig then. Why wasn't he speaking up? He'd just said he was happy here.

Emil held up his hands. "Look, I didn't say we were going yet. I agree that we should at least find these ravageurs and clear them out, okay? But that means you have to stop being so quick to take your temper out on them. We need information, not dead bodies."

Christian grunted and went back to his dinner.

CHAPTER 3

A TINY VILLAGE SOUTH OF PARIS, FRANCE

Christian lifted the last bag of flour off the cart and hefted it onto his left shoulder. The sun caught his eyes as he crossed the street to the bakery, so he had to squint to check his watch. Only 14:30! This was the last stop on the supply run, and they'd make it home before dinner. That meant Christian would have time to check with Grundig and see if he'd uncovered any more clues about where the mysterious ravageur armored car they'd recovered a few days ago.

"Where does this go?" he asked as he entered the bakery, shaking one end of the flour sack.

"This way," Fluse said from a door behind the glass counter. He continued chatting with the baker in French as Christian set the bag down next to two others.

"Thank you," the baker said. He was an older man with a generous paunch and a warm smile. He gestured to a wheel of cheese and a loaf of bread on a nearby table.

Christian made himself at home with a generous hunk of bread and a wedge of cheese. The bread was chewy and had a nutty flavor, better even than the rations the Marauders had in Paris. This bakery had become a regular stop on the southern supply runs for more than just strategic reasons.

"He also has a few extra loaves of bread and some preserves for the food bank in the city," Fluse said.

Christian nodded and smiled. The Marauders were making an impact by ferrying supplies between the villages and the city, even though they still had to stop the ravageurs and the Martians.

Before Christian could get too comfortable, the sound of shouting echoed from the road outside. He shoved the last piece of bread in his mouth and ran to the door.

A man was standing in the middle of the village, holding a small child in his arms and shouting in rapid-fire French. Christian understood two words: *Martian* and *Marcheur*, the French name for Martian Wanderers.

Fluse ran to the man, who was clearly exhausted, and took the child as he spoke to him. Once he finished his conversation and passed the child to a woman, he turned to Christian. "He was visiting family a few kilometers away, and some kind of battle broke out in the woods and spooked his horse," Fluse explained. "Sounds like it was between a Wanderer and some ravageurs?"

"Then let's go," Christian said. "We can take the Panzer."

"We're not out here to engage the enemy. Especially not Martians."

Christian had to admit Fluse was right. Their mission was to deliver supplies, not go in search of battles with Martians or ravageurs. If Emil was here, he'd have them clear out as quickly as possible. But if they caught their enemies in battle with each other, they could teach them a lesson—and get the prisoner that Emil wanted so badly.

"But Emil wants a prisoner," Christian said. "This could be our chance."

"I'm not going to endanger all these men for that," Fluse said.

Another good point, Christian realized. "So send them back. I'll drive the Panzer with you."

Fluse's brow wrinkled.

"We don't get chances like this every day," Christian urged.

"Fine," Fluse said. "But as soon as it looks like we might get in trouble, we're heading back to Paris."

Once they returned to the Panzer, Christian sat down at the fire control station while Fluse piloted the tank out of the village on onto the main road at a brisk thirty-five kilometers per hour. The Panzer was a modern marvel. Powered by a Martian power supply, it never required refueling and made less than half the noise of its previous diesel-powered incarnation. It also boasted a heat ray as its primary weapon, so it could fire without reloading and was faster and more agile without the weight of shells. Grundig had worked with metalworkers in Paris to modify the vehicle tracks and move the power supply into a heavily armored location, making the Panzer safer for its crew.

Still, as Christian peered through the heat ray's crosshairs, he wished the massive war machine moved more rapidly. He wanted to catch the enemy in the act.

They crested a small hill, and Christian spotted a plume of smoke rising from the woods on the road's eastern side. "Over there!" he said over the intercom.

"I see it," Fluse said. Grundig had outfitted the Panzer with a periscope for the driver, but it was hard to imagine how Fluse saw anything over the continuously vibrating system of mirrors.

The Panzer banked in the direction of the woods and headed over an open field, stopping short of the thick tree line. The vehicle fell silent. Soon, nothing other than birds and a light breeze were audible.

"Do you hear anything?" Fluse asked over the intercom.

Christian shook his head. There was no deep thrum of a heat ray. No pop of small weapons fire.

After a few minutes, Fluse opened the Panzer's big crew door and stepped outside. Christian followed, still listening closely. Fluse sniffed the air and made eye contact with him.

Burnt flesh. Christian could smell it, too. A common sign that Wanderers had been near.

"Seems like whatever happened is over," Christian said. "I can scout ahead on foot if you think the Panzer would attract too much attention in the woods."

Fluse nodded. "Be careful."

Christian chambered a round and entered the woods, staying low and making as little noise as possible. The Panzer fell out of sight almost right away as he plunged into the tree cover. After he'd been pushing his way through tree branches and thick foliage for a few minutes, the orange glow of a fire emerged in front of him, and the stench of burning meat became nearly overpowering. Christian tied a handkerchief over his mouth and nose before hurrying onward.

The fire grew brighter as he came to a clearing. At one point, it must have been a ravageur camp. Now it was an abattoir. The fire was really several fires. A tent. A cart. A truck. An automobile.

And a pile of bodies.

Christian wretched. He'd seen enemy soldiers cut down by gunfire while charging across no-man's-land. He'd witnessed men killed by the Black Smoke deployed by the Pioneer Battalions, often indiscriminately, as the German Army had raced across Belgium to the sea. And just a few days ago, he'd seen a heat ray turned on an innocent civilian.

But this was different. Someone had collected the bodies, piled them into macabre mounds, and turned the heat ray on them. Had they already been dead? Or had they been burned alive? And why had the attackers left them burning, rather than turning them to ash?

Something moved out of the corner of Christian's eye. He brought his rifle to his shoulder and got his answer: An arm was sticking out from the closest pile of bodies.

Bile climbed into Christian's throat again. He raised the rifle, ready to fire more out of mercy than anger.

Another arm followed the first one. Eventually, a figure emerged from the pile before slumping onto the ground next to it.

Christian approached the man, his M98 still raised. "Hold it right there."

No response. The man's clothes and skin were burnt on one side. He'd either taken an indirect hit from a heat ray or been close to something else that had.

"Water," the man rasped.

Christian's finger tightened on the trigger. This was a ravageur. An enemy. If he hadn't been lying there burning, he'd be raiding a village.

But whoever he was, did he deserve this? Piled like kindling and set alight?

And Emil wanted a prisoner. Alive. The man didn't have a weapon and wasn't in any condition to use one if he had. Would he make it back to Paris alive?

Christian pulled his canteen off his belt and offered the man a drink. "Can you walk?" he asked.

The man nodded and slowly sat up. Christian helped him to his feet. His burns appeared to be superficial.

"You're from the Marauders," the man said in perfect German.

"Yes, I'm taking you to Paris," Christian said.

The man nodded. He was in no condition to resist. "They came out of nowhere," he said. "Never said a word. Just started lighting us up with their rays."

"You expected the Martians to say something?" Christian asked.

"Martians? No. They had help from the Martians, but this was men. They drove that car." The man pointed to one of the burning vehicles. "It had a heat ray on it. They attacked with a Wanderer."

Christian reeled for a second. This man wasn't from the same group as the one that had attacked Goussainville?

"One of us managed to get that thing with a grenade," the man continued, "but they had three or four of those cars. We didn't have a chance. I played dead. They piled us up and . . ." He broke off into sobs.

So, Christian realized, there was more than one group of ravageurs. And one of them was a bunch of butchers working with Martians.

CHAPTER 4

GOUSSAINVILLE, FRANCE

The horse was found grazing on the same ground Christian had lain upon a few days earlier. With sturdy shoulders and a thick torso, the stallion looked like a well-bred military mount, unlike the lean workhorses Emil and Christian had left tied up in town before walking out to the field. The detailed leatherwork of its saddle was visible from ten meters away. It told Christian that this was a cavalry soldier's mount, not a farmer's horse that might find itself pulling a plow or cart.

Christian and Emil were back in Goussainville to gather intelligence on the ravageurs while the rest of the Marauders were taking a well-deserved day off. It was a risk, but they were only there to poke around, not distribute supplies or stir up trouble.

Their prisoner hadn't had much to offer in terms of intelligence last night. All he knew was that someone from another group had tried to force him and his comrades into an alliance. His leader had refused, and the attack had been the response.

Christian took a deep breath and scanned the area. The ravageurs had never used horses, at least not when they'd attacked. Whose animal was this? And where were they?

"No sign of anyone," Emil said. "Maybe its rider is gone? Injured? Or killed?"

"The villagers said it's been wandering around the area for a couple of hours," Christian replied.

"But why here? Why hasn't it searched for its rider? Or at least wandered closer to the village?"

Then, as if to answer Emil's question, someone appeared at the edge of the woods where the ravageurs had appeared the day before. He wore cavalry breeches and a sword on one hip. His face came into view as he stepped out of the shadows.

Christian's mouth fell open.

"Ritter?" asked Emil, also slack-jawed.

Christian shouldered his rifle. Ritter had been one of Wegener's men. The man had taken them to Reims as de facto prisoners and then disappeared when his leader had been overthrown.

"No," Emil said. "Wait."

Christian kept his sights on Ritter. This man had laughed when Wegener's Panzer had destroyed a Gasthaus full of people in Hermonville. There was no reason to let him live. "For what?" Christian demanded. "You think he's here to share a beer with us? Reminisce about the good old days? He's a Wegener sympathizer."

"If he wanted to kill us, then why would he leave his horse out in the open and walk up to us with no visible back-up?" Emil asked.

"Who cares? Let me kill him."

"Let's see what he wants first. You can always shoot him later."

Emil stepped forward, his hands at his sides. Christian followed with his rifle still raised.

Ritter stopped when they were about ten meters apart. "Tell your man to lower his Mauser, Zimmerman," he said. "This is a diplomatic visit."

Diplomatic? Ritter had always struck Christian as a warrior, not a diplomat.

"Are you alone?" Emil asked Ritter.

"Yes."

Emil nodded to Christian.

"You believe him?" Christian asked.

"He would have killed us by now if he wanted to. He must want to talk."

Christian sighed and lowered his rifle but kept a finger on the trigger. "I hope you're right, Emil."

"Me too."

Ritter closed the distance between them. "I'm not used to seeing you without a cup of coffee," he said.

"I'm not used to seeing you dressed more like a soldier than a circus clown," Emil snapped. "But you've still got the ridiculous pigsticker on your waist. Planning on facing some Mongol hordes this afternoon?"

"You never change," Ritter said, frowning.

"Why would I? Other than toppling your erstwhile kaiser and successfully defending Reims, it's been a short few months." Emil smiled then. He was clearly enjoying himself. "And what have you been up to?"

Ritter pursed his lips, looked away for a moment before answering. "I've been making friends. Friends who asked me to deliver a message to you."

It was Emil's turn to frown. "Friends? Are you the man behind these ravageurs? Maybe I *should* let Beckenbauer put a few rounds in you."

"Ravageurs? That's what you call them? Just a few months in France, and you've gone native. But you like names, don't you? Ludwig's Marauders? How colorful! Who was Ludwig again?"

Emil growled. Christian wasn't sure if he'd have to hold him back—or if he wanted to. But then Emil took a deep breath.

"But no, those common criminals are not my friends," Ritter

went on, smiling. "I've already taken care of most of them south of Paris. I'll be done up here soon, too."

Christian's grip on his rifle tightened so quickly that he nearly fired it into the ground. The stench of burnt flesh still clung to his clothes from the slaughter he'd found yesterday, and he knew he'd have nightmares about that for months. And now Ritter was admitting to being part of that?

"So you're behind those armored cars?" Emil asked, picking up the same hint Christian had. "Your men took out that camp yesterday? Who's building the weapons for you? Can he make them as fast as you're leaving them on the battlefield? Your friends need a military leader who's at least as worried about strategy as he is with his clothes."

Ritter's smiled left as quickly as it had come. "My friends tried to work with Wegener, but he was . . . unreliable. He trusted men like you and Grundig. How is Grundig doing, by the way? Has he betrayed you yet? Or is there honor among thieves?"

Heat rose in Christian's face, and his heart raced. Friends? Ritter was talking about the Martians. The Martians were outfitting those cars. They'd failed when they'd tried to get Wegener to kill humans for them, so they'd hired Ritter instead.

"Your friends?" Christian growled as he raised his weapon. "The aliens? The ones destroying our cities? The ones that wiped out my . . . our families and tried to kill us in the trenches?"

Ritter, to his credit, remained calm. "My friends are inevitable," he said. "They will conquer this planet whether I help them or not. At least I can guarantee a place for myself and whoever I deem worthy."

Emil laughed. "Inevitable? So Reims was part of their plan? To lull us into a false sense of security by losing four of their Wanderers? And now they're sending armored Renaults to be burned by roving bands of thieves? Mein Gott, please ask them to show mercy on us before we die of boredom."

Ritter ground his teeth. "You caught them off guard once.

And even you must realize that Grundig's weapon won't work at scale. Are you going to destroy all the technology on this planet to defeat the aliens?"

Christian knew Ritter was right. Grundig's radioflash could disable all electronics within its range. This meant that the Marauders had to drive their Panzer away from the city in order to use it against the Martians.

"You can have his horse," Christian said as he aimed at Ritter's head.

Ritter took a step back and raised his open palms to his shoulders.

"Wait," Emil said, pushing Christian's rifle back down.

"Wait? For what? You want to talk to this . . . traitor?"

"Kill him and we learn nothing. And I'm sure he lied about being alone." Emil turned back to Ritter. "Tell us whatever you came here to say and then go."

Christian lowered his rifle the rest of the way. Emil had a point. If they were killed, they couldn't get word back to Paris about what was happening.

Ritter eyed both men and crossed his arms. "I had hoped you'd be reasonable," he said evenly. When Emil didn't reply, he sighed before adding, "My friends sent me to make a simple offer. You can keep Paris."

Emil's brow crinkled. "Keep it?"

"We will leave it be. Just play hero in the city, and leave the villages and the men behind those raids to me."

Emil stroked his chin. "And what will your friends do with the villages?"

"That is none of your concern. Paris will remain safe. You can even have a few days to get some villagers to relocate there if it makes you feel better." Ritter smiled again.

Christian's mouth fell open. Ritter wanted to bargain over human lives, and Emil was listening to him? Was he really considering it? "You're not going to make a deal with this—"

Emil cut Christian off with a raised hand.

"This *what*?" Ritter asked. "Killer? Isn't that what you are? You're the sharpshooter who killed Wegener. What makes you different? Your allies?"

"I'm not the same as you!" Christian said, raising the rifle again and nearly striking Ritter in the forehead with it.

Emil stepped in and blocked the rifle. "Isn't this the same agreement they made with Wegener?" he asked. "The deal that led to us having to defend Reims from your friends?"

Ritter dropped his arms to his sides and cast his gaze away again. "As I said, Wegener was unreliable. They expected him to stay in Reims, not make plans to march to Paris."

"We're not giving up our weapons," Emil said.

"My friends aren't asking you to do that. Just stay in the city."

Emil shifted his gaze down to his feet and kicked at a small stone. "I'll need to discuss this with my men and the rest of the leaders in Paris."

"Wonderful. I'm sure Madame Curie and the cardinal will see reason. Have a nice day." Ritter turned away then and walked toward his horse.

"You're considering it?" Christian asked. "Making a deal with them?"

"Not now," Emil said.

"So?" Christian said as he and Emil steered their horses out of the village and toward Paris.

"That was certainly interesting," Emil said.

"Interesting? *Interesting!* Because if they agree to leave Paris alone, you can take us back to Germany and play hero?"

Emil spun around on his saddle to face Christian. "Is that what you think?"

"You've been talking about what they want, and now you're here making deals with a traitor."

"I didn't make a deal."

"You didn't say no, either," Christian growled.

Emil shrugged. "Of course I didn't."

Christian glared at Emil and squeezed the reins so hard that his knuckles went white.

"What would have happened if I said no?" Emil asked.

"He'd know we're not making deals with traitors!"

"And? Is that what's important? What Ritter thinks of us? That he knows we think we're better than him?"

It was now Christian's turn to shrug. "Sure."

"If I said no, they'd start making plans to attack Paris. They might have even tried to kill us on our way home. But since I said I would discuss it with Madame Curie and the cardinal, they'll wait, assuming the deal is genuine in the first place. I bought us some time."

Christian huffed.

"Look," Emil said. "I know we had our differences in Reims. I didn't think we could fight Wegener, and I wanted to give up. You and Ludwig both wanted to stop him, and you were right."

That was what Christian had wanted to hear for weeks. And now that he had, he didn't know what to do or say.

Neither man spoke for a few minutes. Finally, Emil said, "With Ludwig gone, you've become my unofficial second-in-command."

Christian remembered that Ludwig had been Emil's Unteroffizier and served as the Marauders' nominal second-in-command before they'd called themselves the Marauders. Then he'd been killed while saving civilians from a fire during the Battle of Reims. The group's full name was Ludwig's Marauders in his honor.

"I need you to step up," Emil continued. "Act like a leader. And part of that is thinking about the greater good."

And there it was. Emil had finally admitted he'd been wrong about Reims, and now he was justifying making the same mistake here.

"So appeasing Ritter, not to mention the cardinal, is for the greater good?" Christian said.

"We all know how you feel about the church—"

"And that makes whatever I say wrong."

"No. It means you need to take a step back and look at the situation. I don't care about the church one way or the other, and I don't like the cardinal, either. But he has a lot of influence in Paris, and if we alienate him, it'll make it a lot harder for us to help people around here."

"So, the greater good," Christian grumbled.

"Exactly," Emil said.

There was no point in debating Emil about the church. "And Ritter?" Christian asked. "You're going to bring his deal to the city leaders?"

"Of course. I'll say we should tell him to go to hell, but they need to know he's here and trying to get us to stop protecting the villages."

Christian grunted. They should have shot Ritter as soon as they'd been far enough away to avoid any protection he had.

"Christian," Emil said, lowering his voice and making eye contact, "I'd like to make your position as my second-in-command more official. We may be about to start a battle on more than one front. I'll need to be able to delegate. Can I count on you?"

Christian hadn't thought about what he considered mundane military matters like promotions, since they'd fled the trenches. But the idea was gratifying, especially since he'd given Emil so much grief the past couple of days. "What about Fluse?" he asked.

Emil smiled. "He's quite happy working with Grundig, and I'm happy to keep him at arm's length."

"That makes sense. Let me think about it?"

Emil's brow furrowed. It took him a moment before he answered, "Sure. Take your time."

CHAPTER 5

THE MARAUDERS' HEADQUARTERS, PARIS, FRANCE

"So that's the new radioflash?" Emil asked, his eyes wide with surprise. He was standing in Grundig's lab with his hand on a cylinder only a little larger than a wine bottle. The weapon that had saved Reims was the size of a water barrel.

Christian tried to pick up the weapon.

"Don't let the size fool you, Christian," Grundig said. "You'll need at least two men."

Grundig was right. It required both of Christian's hands and was still difficult.

"Yes, Herr Zimmerman," Madame Marie Curie said with a small nod. "Herr Grundig and I have worked out how to safely disassemble the Martian reactors so we can use the fissile material to make smaller power supplies and weapons."

Christian noticed that Madame Curie was still wearing black to mourn her husband, who'd perished when Martians had attacked his train from Brussels a little over a month earlier. She looked haggard, wearing the strain of losing her spouse and running the French Resistance with tired eyes and dark clothes.

"Madame Curie's contributions to the project have been invaluable, Hauptmann," Grundig added. "She's familiar with the safe handling of the material. With this device, we can not only take the battle to the invaders, but we can more easily disable their weapons without sacrificing ours."

The radioflash could create an implosion that disabled all nearby electrical devices. This meant that the Marauders couldn't use their Panzer during the defense of Reims; it would have been ruined when they'd triggered the weapon to stop the Martian Wanderers. That initial version had used an entire Martian power supply, and its effect had covered the entire city. Moreover, firing it had destroyed Wegener's compound and contaminated the nearby fields.

Even with the weapon's considerable weight, the implications of this smaller version were staggering. It was portable and had a smaller range, and they could create more of them.

"This is it," Christian said. "This is what we need to attack Ritter and his 'friends.'"

"We still need to test it," Grundig said. "Based on what we learned in Reims and what the Americans experienced during the Tesla fire, it will contaminate the area around the implosion. We were lucky in Reims, but I'm more optimistic about this design."

"We can arrange a test in the south, then," Emil responded. "The area where you found that ravageur camp will probably work, Christian. How hard are these things to use? Would we be able to train the townspeople? Or set up fuses for them to trigger in the event of an attack?"

"Yes, I can make at least five or six of these for every reactor you can bring me," Madame Curie said. "We should be able to protect the villages that surround the city, and ourselves at the same time. No more defenseless villages leveled by those beasts and their infernal machines."

Madame Curie was right. This was what they needed to take the battle to the enemy.

"We can go on the offensive, too," Christian said. "We can

attack the Martians and use this to get past the ravageur heat rays."

"Not right away," interjected Grundig. "The operator still needs to be at least a few hundred meters away, and behind some kind of cover. This device is very small, but the implosion still has a nasty radius. We also need electrical cable, which has been difficult to find, and setting these weapons takes some planning."

Christian frowned.

"And we don't know how many troops Ritter has, how well he's supplied, or where he is," Emil added. "Shoring up defenses around the perimeter of the city is the most logical first step."

Christian groaned inwardly. Shoring up defenses. Worrying about supplies. The longer they waited, the more of those armored cars Ritter could build. He might even come up with an actual Panzer.

"Have you had any luck with that car we captured?" Emil asked Grundig, almost as if he was reading Christian's mind.

"We have!" Grundig offered one of his unsettling black smiles before coughing. "Over here."

Christian and the others followed him to a table against the far wall. Grundig took a device about the size of a pistol and held it up as if he were starting an auction. It had the familiar polished mirror of a heat ray but was smaller and seemed lighter than anything Christian had seen in the past.

"This weapon has nearly three-quarters the strength of the one mounted on our Panzer but needs less than half the power," Grundig explained. "It's nearly light enough to hold and aim by hand, but still powerful enough to use mounted on a car or Panzer. We can make similar weapons using what we've learned from this, and power the new devices using the cylinders we designed for the smaller radioflash."

Emil stroked his chin for a moment. "So what you're saying is that, given enough supplies, we can finally start producing weapons with interchangeable parts, instead of one-offs?" he asked.

"Yes, genau," Grundig said with another nauseating smile. "More Panzers. More heat rays. More radioflashes."

"Good. We need to keep the news of these new developments quiet. Ritter made a point of rubbing what he knows about us in my face. I think he has at least one informant in our ranks."

"How are we going to test and deploy the new weapons without revealing that they exist?" Christian asked.

"We'll have to keep the circle of people involved small," Emil said.

Christian clenched his fists. The Marauders were finally ready to take the war to the aliens. But was Emil?

CHAPTER 6

PARIS, FRANCE

ities, especially French cities, were filthy places. They reeked of human waste, spoiled food, and mistreated animals. Even worse, they were teeming with inferiors. Foreigners. The filthy streets overflowed with rejects and undesirables. Outlanders. Ritter preferred somewhere that offered more space, cleaner air, and better company.

But Zimmerman's transparent attempt to stall for time hadn't fooled Ritter or his allies. The latest message on the aliens' writing machine had read, "Talk to the cardinal." So, into the city he'd gone.

Crowded cities weren't just dirty. They were dangerous, too, especially for a man who couldn't afford to be seen. Ritter had even more reason to worry about that now that he'd revealed himself to Zimmerman. If word spread that a man who looked like him had visited the cardinal, things would be even more difficult.

A captain of the Third Royal Saxon Hussars, being forced to act as a messenger boy. It was humiliating when Ritter thought about it too much. But giving the invaders what they wanted would mean a place for him after they completed their conquest.

Ritter had spent three days watching and waiting. He'd been

able to track a deer for hours by the time he'd turned ten years old. Following the cardinal's movements around Paris was simply a matter of following a different prey ranging through a different forest.

The cardinal traveled in an elaborate coach that was more fitting for a prince than a holy man. Ritter had been raised as a good Katholisch, but this cardinal was more ostentatious, more entitled, than any man of God he'd ever seen.

The coach was well-guarded and stuck to busy streets, so approaching the cardinal while he traveled was out of the question. Approaching him at the huge cathedral on the Seine would have been equally risky. Ritter needed to have a private conversation with him, away from the prying eyes of civilians and guards alike.

He'd learned that the cardinal valued his privacy and ensured his residence remained isolated. Even the handful of guards that protected it were forbidden from entering the main building. So if Ritter got inside the house, he'd only have to worry about the few servants.

It was four hours after sunset when Ritter scaled the fence and slowly lowered himself into the darkest corner of the expansive yard. He knew the guards kept a regular schedule and cut their perimeter walk short near where he landed. Maybe they didn't know why a religious leader needed armed guards, either.

Ritter weaved his way to a disused side entrance, using a stand of trees, a horse trough, and finally a smokehouse as cover. Soon, he was inside a darkened entrance foyer. He brushed off dirt and leaves from his pants, straightened his tunic, and surveyed the house.

As near as he could tell during his surveillance, the cardinal had three live-in servants. Their quarters were on the far side of the residence, adjacent to the kitchen. Ritter removed his boots, walked through the sitting room, and approached the stairs to the second floor. They brought him to a spacious hallway decorated with oil paintings and fine carpeting.

He continued down the hall, hugging the wall, until he reached double doors that opened into a master bedroom. The room was cavernous. In Reims, Wegener had assuaged his ego by building a larger and larger command post as the weeks had passed. The entire structure would have fit comfortably in this room, with space to spare for the enormous bed and garish furnishings.

Wegener would have been better off occupying the Reims cathedral.

The cardinal was sleeping on his back, his enormous belly forming a mountain under his comforter. He was snoring—a loud, gagging, vile sound that was intense enough to hurt one's ears.

Ritter sat down in an overstuffed chair that rested against a wall near the bed. He pulled a pistol from his jacket and rested it on his left knee. Then he produced a cigar, carefully cut off the tip, lit it, and started puffing.

Within a few minutes, the cardinal broke into a coughing fit and sat up, choking. He took a few deep breaths before his eyes fell on Ritter.

"Move or shout, and I'll put one between your eyes," Ritter said in French, holding up the pistol with his right hand before taking a long, luxurious puff from the cigar.

"Who are you?" the cardinal grumbled. "How did you get in here? I'll kill those worthless guards." He gagged again before he could say more.

"I'll ask the questions," Ritter said.

"Where are you from?" the cardinal said in perfect German. "Your French is terrible."

Ritter sat back in surprise for a moment, then brought the gun back to bear on the cardinal. "I said I'll ask the questions," he said in German this time. "You're German? Bavarian, from the sound of it?"

"I was born in Regensburg. And you must be Prussian. A

soldier? Or at least you were, before you started robbing churches."

"Robbing?" Ritter stuck out his chin. "I'm no common thief. I'm here to talk business. The kind of business that will keep you alive."

"Excuse me. A blackmailer, then."

This man was accustomed to being in control. That needed to change. Ritter needed a Soldat, not a Leutnant. "That's enough," he said. "What is the nature of your relationship with Emil Zimmerman and his Marauders?"

"The nature? What do you mean?"

"Answer me." Ritter waved the gun as a reminder. "You're right. I'm a soldier, and your guards are incompetent. I can kill you and walk out of here."

The cardinal raised his hands in defense. "Emil Zimmerman is an ally. Nothing more. A tool, really. He helps distribute supplies and Bibles to the villages," He turned to dangle his feet over the edge of his bed. They didn't reach the floor.

"Does he provide any support for you inside the city? Help guard the cathedral?"

The cardinal's brow furrowed. "No. What's this all about?"

Ritter leaned back in the chair and took another puff from the cigar, wishing he had a snifter of brandy to go with it. Given all the opulence surrounding the cardinal, it was surprising there wasn't one next to the chair.

The cardinal cleared his throat and stood up. Ritter nearly dropped his cigar in surprise before leaning forward in the chair and raising the gun again. "I didn't tell you to stand!" he hissed.

"If you're going to interrogate me, I'll need a drink of water." The cardinal walked to his dresser, filled a tumbler from a pitcher of water, and took a long drink. "So, what do you want to talk about?"

Ritter reeled in his seat. Either this man truly thought God was on his side, or ice water ran through his veins.

Before Ritter could answer him, footsteps sounded on the stairs and started down the hall.

"You're going to tell them you're okay," Ritter whispered, "or I'll make sure they die before I kill you."

The cardinal shrugged.

Someone tried the locked door, then knocked. "Are you all right, Your Grace?" asked a tremulous voice in French.

"Yes, I'm fine," the cardinal said. "I merely stumbled coming back from the privy."

"Are you sure, Your Grace?"

"I said I'm okay. Go back to sleep!" The cardinal's voice had an edge to it now.

The hall was silent for a few seconds, then footsteps sounded again, growing fainter as the servant reached the stairs and descended.

"Very good," Ritter said once the footsteps were out of range. "Now, listen to me. The church isn't going to send supplies to the villages anymore."

The cardinal's brow wrinkled. He tilted his head, as if thinking for a moment, before asking, "Are you interested in the Marauders? Or in cutting off supplies to the villages? Are you from some sort of rival mercenary group? I don't think Zimmerman's been collecting money from the villagers, unless he's managed to do it without me finding out."

"What? No!" Ritter sputtered. This man was convinced he was some kind of common criminal.

"Well, whatever you're up to, you must be new to it." The cardinal poured himself another glass of water. "I'd offer you some water, but I only have one glass. I'm not used to entertaining up here. And here, use this for your ashes." He picked up a saucer and approached Ritter, as if to hand it to him.

Ritter took the saucer and tipped his cigar into it before realizing the cardinal was giving him orders.

"So, you don't want the Marauders heading out into the villages anymore," the cardinal went on. "You—or, more likely, someone you work for—wants control of them, and the Marauders and their Panzers are in the way. But you asked about Zimmerman first, didn't you?"

Ritter frowned.

"You're both from the German Army," the cardinal added. "Or, more precisely, were. Maybe you're acquainted with each other? Rivals? Estranged friends?"

"Something like that," Ritter said.

"What do I get in return for my cooperation?"

So that was why he was convinced Ritter was after money. The cardinal was a criminal, so he saw the same in everyone else. A threat would probably only last until Ritter left the room.

"We're prepared to leave Paris alone," Ritter said.

"For now, at least," the cardinal said as Ritter inhaled on his cigar. "You're working with the aliens, then."

Ritter coughed.

"That's it!" The cardinal pointed at Ritter. "Zimmerman spoke of a group of collaborators he came up against in Reims. He thought he'd stopped all of you. But he hasn't, has he?"

Ritter stayed silent. He didn't see any reason to correct the inaccuracies in that theory.

The cardinal crossed his arms. "Well, I've never been sure that the Resistance has a chance against them, especially with that witch Curie in charge, and I have no loyalty to Zimmerman and his men. You can have the villages, but in return for making things easier for you, I want a seat at the table when they finally come for Paris."

"Why not just kill you now?" Ritter asked. "Or later?"

"Because I do a lot more than just shut down the supply lines. I can keep Zimmerman's Marauders busy in Paris, too."

CHAPTER 7

THE MARAUDERS' HEADQUARTERS, PARIS, FRANCE

f Emil had mentioned that being second-in-command would mean attending weekly meetings, Christian would have refused the offer outright. But here he was, not even official yet, sharing a table in the mess with Emil, Grundig, Fluse, and Madame Curie.

The other four were discussing strategy, logistics, and politics. Christian, however, was thinking about the actual work he could be doing, like scouting for Martians, locating and delivering food and water to the villages, or rolling socks into neat little balls the way his Unteroffizier in basic training liked.

"The test was a resounding success," Grundig said. "The unit destroys an area of about fifty square meters, but the magnetic pulse covers about four times as much."

"How quickly can you start making them?" Emil asked as he poured himself coffee from the French press he'd brought from the mess hall.

"With the people you've approved bringing into the circle, we can have fifteen or so units ready in about a week," Madame Curie said.

"That's fine. No reason to risk bringing anyone else in."

"If we work quickly enough, Ritter's informant—assuming they really exist—won't make a difference," Christian said. "And if we figure out where he and his 'friends' are hiding, we can use the new devices and the new heat rays to wipe them out."

"You're in a hurry to drag us into a direct confrontation," Emil said.

"I'm in a hurry to make the traitors pay," Christian said.

Grundig shot Christian a look. Christian only frowned before adding, "I witnessed his men killing innocent civilians. I saw what they did to the other ravageur group. No one deserves to die like that."

"No one except him, of course," Emil said with a wry smile.

"You know what I mean."

"I know, but I'm not sure you do. But we have more important issues. The church is having difficulty with supplies. We have nothing to distribute."

"This can't be a coincidence," Christian said.

"What do you mean?" Fluse asked.

"Ritter tells us to withdraw into the city, and a week later there's no supplies?" Christian held his hands up in wonder.

"You've made your opinion about the church abundantly clear," Fluse said. "Now you're accusing it of being in league with Ritter and the Martians? The cardinal negotiated peace between the street gangs rioting over on the left bank of the Seine last week."

And there it was. Yes, Christian hated the church, and the opportunity to prove the Marauders didn't need them was appealing. But that didn't mean his ideas weren't worth considering.

Heat rose in his cheeks. "Here we go again," he said, struggling to keep his voice level. "I don't like the church, so whatever I say must be wrong."

"Nobody said that," Emil said. "But we already believe Ritter has an informant in the Marauders. So now you think he has someone in the church, too? He'll have the whole city working for him before winter."

"No, not exactly," Christian said. "But you don't think it's possible the cardinal might be involved? Or at least someone close enough to him that they could interrupt the supplies?"

"I think it's more likely Ritter is interfering with his supply chain." Emil answered as he poured himself another cup.

"Then why doesn't the church ask us to help him fix it?" Christian asked.

"Because we've never been on great terms with them," Fluse said. "You're accusing the cardinal of relinquishing entire villages to the aliens."

Seeing Fluse take Emil's side was infuriating. A few months ago, he'd have jumped at the chance to disagree with him. Now, he was piling onto Christian.

"What if he is?" Madame Curie asked. She had been characteristically silent during the meeting so far, so all eyes fell on her when she finally spoke. Even in this dusty factory-turned-military base and surrounded by soldiers, it was clear she was a leader and commanded respect.

"What do you mean?" Emil asked.

"What can we do? Confront him? Unseat him? Kill him? Take the supplies by force? Find out where he gets them from and take them ourselves?" Madame Curie shrugged then.

Christian knew she was no fan of the church. There was bad blood between them, dating back to Paris's rebuilding efforts after the first Martian Attack. The Curies had been critical in the city's restoration, spearheading the creation of a public electric grid and pushing hard for housing for workers. The church had opposed both, pointing to the Tesla fire in New York City as proof that electricity was a curse from Satan and stating that free housing presented the average "uneducated worker" with a moral hazard.

The church had always enjoyed a strong voice in France, but its position had grown stronger after the first Martian Attack.

Notre-Dame Cathedral had been left intact, a circumstance the cardinal had declared a "miracle and a message from God." He'd tried to use the circumstances to create a theocracy and come dangerously close to succeeding.

"I don't trust the cardinal for obvious reasons," Madame Curie went on, "but I'm not sure he'd go as far as working with the Martians. That said, the villages rely on us. We need to help them regardless of why they're in trouble."

"Exactly!" Christian exclaimed. "It's been three weeks since the church has provided us with anything. The people have run out of flour up north, and two of the southern villages are having problems keeping their cattle fed. We could at least shuttle some supplies between them."

Madame Curie nodded. "That's a good idea."

"While we do that, we can investigate how the church got their supplies," Fluse said. "Even if the cardinal isn't lying, we may be able to solve the problem."

Emil took a long drink of coffee and looked down into his mug for a moment before saying, "I suppose we can think about redistributing supplies between the villages, but we need to stay focused on monitoring the Martians." He looked to Fluse. "And you just volunteered to look into whether the cardinal has been truthful with us."

Fluse nodded.

"Where are we on the new heat rays and Panzers?" Emil asked.

"The Renault will be done tomorrow," Grundig said.

"Is this the prototype light model we found in that armaments factory?" Emil asked.

"Yes. It needed a lot of work, but it's ready, and the lighter heat ray we got from the car is mounted and ready to go. This Panzer is nearly as fast as an automobile now."

"What about the British Panzer we recovered from the battlefield up north?" Christian asked.

"We're still having problems with the power train." Grundig

shrugged. "The thing weighs much more than our German model."

Emil nodded and took another sip of coffee. "Still no word from the French military, Madame Curie?" he asked.

"Nothing at all," she replied. "It seems like they fared as well as they did in the first Attack."

"Maybe it's time to talk to Berlin again," Emil said. "See if we can work out some kind of agreement with them."

Christian's jaw dropped. This again? "If you talk to them, they're just going to order you to return to Germany," he said.

"We don't know that. They may be able to offer support somehow. You're the one who wants to take the battle to the Martians. Why wouldn't you be interested in getting more troops?"

"Because they're not going to send them here. They're going to tell you to go there."

Emil shrugged. "I can try to make them understand that fighting the aliens is just as important here as it is there."

"You can try," Fluse said. "But if you fail, you're putting yourself in the position of disobeying orders."

That was uncharacteristically candid advice from Fluse. The Leutnant had been a strict military man back in the trenches. Hearing him advise Emil on how to avoid an order he didn't want was a bit of a shock for Christian.

"We are German soldiers, though," Emil said. "And so is Ritter. They may be interested in helping us stop him."

Christian took a deep breath and fought back the urge to shout. Emil had already spoken to Berlin twice so far, and they had all but ordered him to bring the Marauders back to Germany. Why would they be willing to send troops here instead?

The Marauders had survived—no, *thrived*—on their own so far. They needed to stop Ritter and the Martians, not waste time persuading the Army that had been killing them with their own Black Smoke a few months ago to help.

Christian wasn't going to go back to Germany, regardless of who Emil spoke to and what they said. If he had to desert the Marauders to stay here, he would.

CHAPTER 8
NOISY-LE-SEC, FRANCE

t was a blistering summer morning in Noisy-le-sec, a small village east of Paris, and Christian was wasting time unloading verdammt Bibles. He spied a wagon loaded with compost sat on the far side of the town square. Just a few short steps and the books would be put to good use.

The cardinal had refused all invitations to meet in person or collaborate on fixing their supply issues, but Emil had still insisted that they carry his cargo. That didn't mean it had to go to townspeople, though.

Christian hefted a few of the Bibles, then turned to find himself facing Fluse.

"Why don't you move the cart closer to the chapel?" Fluse asked.

"Uhhh . . ."

Screams and shouts resounded behind Fluse just then, sparing Christian from coming up with an excuse. He dropped the books in a heap on the end of the cart and ran toward the crowd of animated villagers. Fluse fell in behind him.

When they reached the crowd, Christian noticed that all eyes were on a red-faced man pointing down the primary road and outside the village. Fluse raised his voice to get the crowd under control and spoke to them in hurried tones. It reminded Christian that he needed to ask Fluse to teach him some more French.

"Ravageurs, with at least one Wanderer, a few kilometers that way," Fluse told him, pointing northeast.

"Let's go," Christian said.

Fluse shook his head. "Not this time. Emil was clear. Deliver supplies and take note if we see or hear anything, but stay out of trouble."

Miller, who was striding up to the group as Fluse spoke, nodded in agreement.

Christian clenched his fists. This was a golden opportunity to take the battle to Ritter and the aliens, and instead they were reciting the rules to him. "We have two Panzers this time," he said, "plus a heat ray on my cart. We've yet to capture anyone with useful intelligence."

"You know how the chain of command works," Miller said.

Fluse nodded and crossed his arms.

Great. Miller and Fluse were together on this.

Maybe Christian should have accepted the offer of a promotion so he'd have more leverage with these martinets. A bead of sweat trickled down his forehead. "I was right the last time," he growled.

"You were lucky. I know you're upset, but Emil knows what he's doing—"

Christian didn't have time for this.

He turned and ran. Miller had driven the Renault today. It was parked near the cart, and if he was over there lecturing, it was unattended.

And there it was, with its front entry door hanging open. Apparently, Miller wasn't so clear on the rules when it came to securing his vehicle.

Christian jumped in, closing and latching the door behind him in a smooth motion. He'd never driven this vehicle before, but like all the other Marauders, he'd had a quick lesson in how to drive the larger German vehicle. How different could it be?

"Beckenbauer!" Fluse bellowed. "Get out of that Panzer right now!" He banged on the door. Hopefully, Christian wouldn't run him over.

Grundig had outfitted the French Panzers with levers similar to the German model. Christian tugged on them, and the vehicle lurched backward a few centimeters. One of the men outside yelped, but seemed more in surprise than pain. Christian checked the driver's periscope and could just barely spot Fluse and Miller off to the side, shaking their fists in anger. He gently moved the levers forward, and the vehicle eased forward to the northern end of town.

He accelerated as soon as he knew he was clear of bystanders. The Renault was fast, which made sense given Grundig's assertions about its weight compared to the German model. It was more maneuverable, too, which tracked with the vehicle's shorter length.

Would Fluse and Miller follow in the heavier fighting machine? There was no way they'd open fire on him. Even if they were angry enough to treat him as a mutineer, they wouldn't risk destroying the Marauder's newest weapon. Hopefully, they'd end up drawn into the battle Christian was hoping to start with the ravageurs.

He checked the compass mounted on the control cluster in front of him. The road was taking him northeast. With luck, it would take him right to the enemy. But was he driving this Panzer to its destruction—and his own death?

Fine. Just as long as he took some of the ravageurs with him.

The road snaked through woods for a few kilometers, then emptied into a clearing where a village came into sight. Christian blinked as he made out the silhouette of a Wanderer. He stopped the Panzer and grabbed the sights and firing control for the heat ray. Hopefully it, too, operated like the one in the other fighting vehicle.

He struck the Wanderer with his first shot. Smoke rose from its side, but it still spun around to face him. He slammed the

Panzer into reverse, and it shot back into a nearby stand of trees, throwing him from his seat and causing his head to strike the door.

Shaking his head to clear it, he scrambled back into the driver's seat and drove the Panzer to the far side of the trees. A trickle of blood ran down his forehead as the hum of a heat ray sounded from outside. The Wanderer was firing at him, but it had missed so far.

He found the Wanderer in the heat ray's sights and fired again, shouting as he held the trigger down and waited for the Wanderer to burst into flames. The temperature gauge for the heat ray climbed into the red zone, and he released the trigger.

Nothing. Only some carbon scoring on the side of the alien craft as it brought its aiming mirror to bear. They'd upgraded their armor somehow!

Christian's heart jumped into his throat. He spun the Panzer to one side and dodged another blast. His mind raced as he plowed through more trees. If he ran, he'd lead the Martians back to the next village—or to Paris. If he was killed, he'd take the Marauders' newest weapon with him.

He drove the Panzer into a thicket and dared another look through the periscope. A car, armored and outfitted with a heat ray, was visible now.

He'd have to focus on one target at a time. Just like he'd been taught in basic training.

Christian focused his attention on the Wanderer. It was painted with a green-and-brown camouflage pattern, like the ones that had attacked the 109th Reserve Regiment back on the Somme. But something was different. The paint had a reflective quality to it. Was it as simple as that? Was it a finish that blunted the effect of the heat rays?

The armored car speeding toward him broke Christian out of his reverie. He shifted to the ray's targeting system and opened fire on the car. It veered off to one side and collided with a building.

That was easy. Ritter's armored car drivers seemed to lack training, like they either expected no resistance or were intended to be nothing more than cannon fodder.

The shot had exposed Christian's position, so he powered the Panzer back out of the thicket and into the open, hoping the vehicle's uncharacteristic speed surprised the Wanderer. He shot past it and darted behind a building. The Wanderer's heat ray hummed to life, trailing him.

Christian powered the Panzer to the far end of the building and stopped just far enough that he could peek out the periscope. The Wanderer had paused, its aiming mirror brandished out front, scanning for a target.

This was Christian's first time facing off with a Wanderer by himself, but it was far from his first encounter. The Marauders had been involved in many skirmishes since that fateful day on the Somme, and they'd learned a lot.

The primary lesson had been that Martians had poor eyesight and excellent hearing. So Christian knew to expect the Martians to do two things: stop and listen for their opponent; then fire sustained, sweeping bursts to make up for poor targeting.

So if the Wanderer couldn't see him from where he was stopped, he had time to work out a strategy, assuming he had disabled the armored car.

The Wanderer's tentacles gleamed in the setting sun. Were they treated with the same finish as the body? Wanderers had two sets of tentacles: thin, supple "arms" used for carrying gear like heat ray emitters and cages; and thicker, stronger "legs" that they walked on. The number of each type varied from one Wanderer to another, but the appendages had always been reflective. That didn't mean they were resistant to heat rays, though. No one had ever targeted them because the body was the obvious target.

Christian aimed for the joint between the body and the closest leg. The Wanderer spun around to face him, but he kept the ray focused on his target.

The tentacle broke away from the Wanderer's body, causing the Wanderer to sprawl to the ground. But it brought two of its thinner "arms" down to the ground to lift itself, then fired its heat ray at the Panzer as it limped away.

The cockpit immediately heated up as Christian pulled the Panzer out of the line of fire. The Renault's armor wasn't as thick as the German model. But he'd figured out how to make the aliens pay.

He shifted back into view and opened fire again, quickly cutting off another limb. The craft stumbled, using two more arms but fleeing with more difficulty this time.

Christian opened the Panzer's throttle to follow, opening fire on a third "leg." The Wanderer shuttered and bounced on the ground as it struggled to use its weaker, thinner limbs to walk.

At the first orphanage the church had put Christian in, there'd been a boy who'd tortured flies by pulling off their legs and wings. The other kids had steered clear of him. Was whatever Christian was feeling now how that boy had felt when terrorizing his victims?

The brutal dance went on for a few more minutes. Eventually, the Wanderer sat disabled on the ground, smoke pouring out from the joints where its tentacles had been.

Christian opened fire with the heat ray, blasting it for a few minutes at a time until it finally burst into flames.

He'd done it. It had been close, and he nearly lost it all. But he'd defeated a Wanderer on his own in face-to-face combat.

Christian raced the Panzer over to the crashed armored car, mentally confirming there was a round chambered in his M98. Slowly, he opened the Panzer door. A shot rang out, and a bullet ricocheted right next to his head. He dropped to the ground and crawled to the far side of his vehicle.

Then he heard someone groan.

Christian peeked around the corner. The barrel of an M98 like his was inching across the grass near the wrecked car. After a moment, a soldier came into view. He was struggling to crawl, with a grimace of pain that was clear on his face, even from fifteen meters away.

He looked familiar. Had he been one of Wegener's men?

Christian spotted cover behind some hedges, then ran to it as the soldier was distracted by his leg. The soldier pulled himself along painfully, stopping when he found what he thought was a safe vantage point. But his judgment was clearly hampered by his injury.

Suddenly Christian realized how he knew this man. They'd met in Reims. He was Schmidt, one of the men assigned to Emil's salvage detail. Was he working for Ritter now?

Christian brought the rifle sight up to his eye. One clean shot, and another one of Ritter's traitors would pay. Schmidt was a seasoned soldier, too. He'd spot Christian soon, once his head cleared.

The Marauders needed a prisoner, though, and there was a good chance they could learn something from Schmidt. Emil knew him, too; he might be able to get him to talk.

But why? Why bring a traitor back to headquarters and give him medical care and precious food?

Christian put the sights on Schmidt's head. It would be so easy.

That was when he lowered his weapon. "I have you covered," he said, "Throw your weapon toward me, and you'll live to see tomorrow."

Schmidt threw his rifle aside and strained to raise his hands.

"Are you alone?" Christian asked.

"Yes," Schmidt growled. "You killed my partner, you bastard."

Christian slowly came out from behind the Panzer, hoping the other soldier was telling the truth. He scooped up Schmidt's rifle. "You work for Ritter now," he said.

"And you still work for that Schwein, Zimmerman," Schmidt said between clenched teeth.

CHAPTER 9

THE MARAUDERS' HEADQUARTERS, PARIS, FRANCE

Christian watched as Emil entered the converted basement supply room and reeled back in shock. "Schmidt!" Emil said.

"There you are, you Schwein," Schmidt hissed. His eyes burned through Emil like a heat ray. "You traitor. Are you a French citizen yet?" He strained against the ropes that kept him in his chair, which flexed as he struggled. Schmidt was only a little taller than Emil but was built like a brick outhouse.

"Why is he tied up like that?" Emil asked.

"He broke Wechsler's nose," Christian said.

"He has a broken leg!"

"Tell Wechsler that."

Emil faced Schmidt, crossed his arms, and shook his head. "You disappeared after Reims," he said. "I figured you'd gone back to Berlin."

"You're the deserter, not me," Schmidt said, grunting as he pushed against the ropes.

"So you went with Ritter? How many others are with you?"

"Do I look like I just fell off the turnip wagon?" Schmidt sneered.

Emil shrugged. "It was worth a try. Besides, you're working with the Martians and calling *me* a traitor? Are you sure you're not being naive? Twenty years ago, they were using us for food, and now they're your allies?"

Schmidt turned away in his chair.

"You're turning their weapons on people," Emil went on. "Villagers! But I'm a traitor? Ritter is worse than Wegener ever was."

Schmidt opened his mouth to speak, then turned away again.

"Has he had any food or water?" Emil asked.

Christian shook his head.

"Get him something."

"I just told you, he attacked us," Christian said.

Emil gestured for Christian to leave the room. They walked out together, and Emil closed the door behind them. "Bring him some food, untie him at gunpoint if need be, then lock him in alone so he can eat," he said. "Or feed him yourself, if you don't want to remove the ropes. We're going to have to figure out how to handle him, or things are going to get messy very soon."

"We're not equipped to handle prisoners!" Christian said.

"We did fine with the first one you brought in," Emil said.

"But he had burns! And he was scared out of his wits."

"Work. It. Out. *You* disobeyed orders and brought him here. It's up to *you* to figure out how to make a silk purse out of this sow's ear." Emil started walking away then.

"So I should have killed him?" Christian asked. "Don't think I didn't consider it!"

Emil turned to face Christian. "Come and find me when you're done. We need to talk."

"I'm not a military man, Christian," Emil began.

They were in Emil's office now, a room that overlooked the factory's courtyard. Emil was seated behind the massive oak desk that had belonged to the factory's owner, and Christian sat across from him. It was like his first job interview at the construction company where he'd worked until the war. But this was a dressing-down, not a new opportunity.

Emil steepled his fingers, his elbows on the desk. "Maybe you remember this from after we left the Somme. Running this group was the last thing I wanted, but I finally realized what had to be done. You helped me with that. Now I need your help again."

Was Christian here for a reprimand? Or was it actually an interview for a new job?

"We spoke about you stepping up and taking a larger role as second-in-command. Since then, you've distinguished yourself as an expert in disobeying orders and stealing Panzers." Emil gave him a rueful smile.

"Yes," Christian interjected. "I'm the Panzer thief who's brought in our only two prisoners and learned about the Martian's tougher armor."

"But at what risk? You took our only two Panzers into combat, with no planning and no backup. The first time, you at least took the time to coerce Fluse into joining you. But the second time, you literally stole the vehicle and charged into a firefight alone. What would have happened if you failed? I would have lost the Panzer *and* you." Emil's voice cracked slightly with that last sentence.

Emil really wasn't a military man. In a functioning army, Christian would have been up on charges and facing prison time. On the battlefield, he might have gotten a firing squad. But here, he was sitting in a rather comfortable chair, listening to his commanding officer try to restrain himself while facing the prospect of losing him.

Of course, it made sense. Emil had been up on charges for attacking an officer the day he and Christian had met.

"You're right," Christian said. "It was an unacceptable risk, and I was lucky."

"At least you can admit that," Emil said. "Look, of all the

men here, you might have the best reason to hate the aliens. Most of us lost someone. I lost my little sister and one of my best friends. But you . . . you lost your whole family. I understand."

Christian felt the heat rise in his cheeks. He started to choke up, but Emil continued before he could respond. "We all want to stop them and the bastards working with them as much as you do. But we'll only manage that together. I don't want to run an army, but I do want to help with an effort to take our world back."

"Then why are you talking to Berlin?" Christian asked. "Why respond to them at all?"

"Because they have supplies. They have the numbers. Because being pragmatic is more effective than being angry. At least some of the men over there are more interested in defeating the aliens than building a new German—"

"Wait!" Emil jumped to his feet then. "That's it! That's the angle!"

Christian leaned back in shock.

"How much do you want to bet that Ritter's been talking to them?" Emil asked.

"Not a single Pfennig," Christian said as he stood up. "He's working with the aliens."

"Of course. But Schmidt called us *traitors*. We worked with him. We know him. He's loyal to Germany. He bought Wegener's story about a new German Empire and all that." At that, Emil held up his hands.

"Then why is he working with Ritter and the aliens?"

"Because Ritter must have fed him some kind of story."

Christian tilted his head. "What kind of story?"

"Doesn't matter. I just know it won't involve Berlin." Emil pounded his fist into his other hand. "I'll put him on the radio with Central Command, if I have to. That'll show him he's working with the wrong people."

He stepped toward the door, then stopped. "I'm not sure I

could promote you now if you wanted it. What kind of example would that set?"

"There's still Fluse. I'd work for him."

Emil shook his head. "We'll see. Consider yourself repri-manded. Let's see what we can learn from Schmidt now that we have a way to approach him."

CHAPTER 10
PARIS, FRANCE

"She's special, Christian," Bumpkin said with a broad smile as Christian drove the cart through Paris on their way home from a supply run. "I'm telling you, she's not just any other girl."

Even with the encircling Martians and the interrupted supply lines, Paris was still the city of love. Bumpkin had met a girl at one of the many bakeries that dotted the area around the Marauders' headquarters, and now Christian felt like he knew her, too. He knew her name was Charlotte, she worked at a local laundry, her father had acres of farmland in the north before the latest invasion, her mother was gone, and her nose looked like the cutest little button.

Christian knew everything there was to know about Charlotte—and because of that, he was a little nauseous. He had also learned that Bumpkin's real name was Otto, although all the Marauders still called him Bumpkin.

The cart rumbled along the cobblestones, providing a soothing background to Otto's story about his latest dinner with Charlotte. There was an adorable way to eat spaghetti, it seemed, and that was how she did it.

Shots echoed from down the boulevard then, startling the men and sparing Christian any further maudlin.

"I'll run ahead," Otto said.

"No," Christian said. "Those shots were well ahead. We have supplies with us, and this convoy has two heat rays that might interest some enterprising gang members."

They were still on the left bank of the Seine, about a kilometer from the crossing to headquarters. The gangs had never attacked a Marauder convoy before, but with the church's supply lines frozen, Christian didn't want to take any risks.

"Prep the heat ray," he said. "I'll pull over so the Panzer can move to the front."

He guided the cart to one side of the street, and Fluse drove the armored vehicle ahead to lead the convoy. The group continued forward, slower this time. The Panzer turned a corner and stopped as another burst of shots rang out.

They'd driven right into a gang war.

The carts turned and pulled back a few hundred meters as the Panzer edged with them and turned to one side, keeping itself between the horses and the gunfire.

"Stay with the cart," Christian said, jumping down to the street with his rifle off his shoulder and a round in the chamber.

The back door of the Panzer opened, and Fluse stepped out as Christian and three others clustered between the armored vehicle and the carts.

"I guess we wait this out," Fluse said. "It might be a distraction, though—"

The sound of horses screaming interrupted him as a cart equipped with a heat ray rode away from the group. Two men had climbed onto it and were frantically trying to maneuver it away from the Marauders.

"Who left that cart alone?" Fluse shouted.

"I thought you were staying with it!" Miller said, pointing at one of the other Marauders.

Miller wasn't very good at keeping an eye on his vehicles, was he?

But now was not the time for finger-pointing. Christian shouldered his weapon, got a bead on the man with the reins, and fired. The man slumped, and the cart slowed. Christian sighted the other man.

"No!" Fluse shouted. "No reason for more than one man to die."

Christian lowered his weapon and raised an eyebrow. No reason? But they'd tried to get away with a heat ray.

Fluse pointed then. Three Marauders were already on the cart, restraining the survivor. "Problem solved," Fluse said. "And now we might find out why they've suddenly changed their tactics."

Miller, on the other hand, was less forgiving. He had the erstwhile thief by his collar and was shaking him hard enough that his head might snap off. After a few moments, the other Marauders managed to calm Miller down, while the gang member cowered on the ground.

"Tie him up and get him back to headquarters," Fluse said. "Meanwhile, that gun battle around the corner seems to have been more than a distraction. Let's see if we can stop them before they destroy the entire neighborhood."

Fluse really had transformed from the team's punching bag into an effective leader—and a good officer. He had protected the convoy with his Panzer and prevented an unnecessary shooting, and now he was prepared to intervene in a riot that might kill civilians. Why hadn't Emil simply made him his executive officer?

One of the Marauders rode off with the prisoner, while Fluse and the others went back to the Panzer to view the ongoing gun battle. Grundig had outfitted the Panzer with a public address system for making announcements during supply deliveries—and in case the Marauders needed to manage evacuations in anticipation of a Martian Attack. Riot control hadn't been on their minds back then, but here they were.

"Attention!" Fluse announced in French through the PA system. "Attention! Cease firing immediately. You are endangering innocent civilians. Cease firing, or we will be forced to intercede."

A single bullet ricocheted off the front of the Panzer in response.

Christian found some cover and peered through his sights, wishing that he'd taken the time to fit his rifle with a telescope. Two groups were doing most of the shooting, from buildings on either side of the embattled city street. He had a clear line of sight on both and could end this with a handful of shots.

He took a bead on one of them and squeezed the trigger. Then, at the last second, he pulled his shot high, sending the men scrambling for cover.

Fluse made his announcement again. Three rounds hit the Panzer this time. He exited the vehicle and returned to Christian and the other Marauders.

"They're not stupid," he grumbled. "I can't use my heat ray without setting the entire left bank of the Seine alight."

Christian swung his sights to the other side of the street and searched for a target.

"Halt!" cried a voice from down the street. "Halt! Stop this immediately and go home!"

It was the monseigneur, walking down the middle of the street with both arms raised as if they could repel the bullets. "Halt!" he continued. "Halt! Stop shooting now!"

The street fell silent then.

"Go home!" the monseigneur shouted. "Go home now, before you kill anyone else."

The windows emptied. The gangs had all disappeared.

Fluse laughed. "That was all it took?"

"The church," Miller growled. "They respect the church more than they respect us."

The monseigneur approached the Panzer and the Marauders then. "So, now you men are part of this madness with the gangs?" he bellowed, his customary smile replaced with a deep frown.

"They attacked us," Fluse said. "This may have been a ruse to steal a weapon."

"What makes you so sure they were after that?" Miller asked.

"They don't need to steal carts or horses," Christian said. "At least not from armed soldiers. They were after the heat rays."

Miller grunted and turned away from them.

"If those weapons weren't here, they wouldn't have anything to steal," the monseigneur growled.

"If our weapons weren't here, Paris would be offering fine French dining for the Martians," Christian snarled, pushing through the Marauders to get close enough to smell the church leader's aftershave.

Fluse put a hand on Christian's chest to restrain him. "We were on our way back from bringing supplies to one of the villages, Monseigneur," Fluse answered. "We didn't start this. We were only pulled in when two men tried to steal our cart."

"Supplies?" the monseigneur asked. "From where?"

"We've developed some of our own sources," Christian said.

"Hmph. I'll need to tell the cardinal about that."

"You do what you have to," Fluse said. "And so will we."

CHAPTER 11

THE MARAUDERS' HEADQUARTERS, PARIS, FRANCE

"We're going to have to hire guards and open a prison soon," Emil said, grinning.

Christian had joined Fluse, and Grundig in Emil's office the day after the skirmish with the gangs. Emil had asked them to meet him there "for coffee" after breakfast. He'd been holding a ten-cup French press and told the men to grab mugs, a clear sign that the invitation wasn't exactly optional.

"Did you learn anything from Schmidt?" Fluse asked.

"Quite a bit," Emil answered. "He loosened up rather quickly after I told him about my discussions with Berlin." He nodded at Christian. "Ritter has been telling his men that Germany collapsed and that they're its last chance to rebuild."

"And they're starting by harassing small villages in the French countryside with the help of alien invaders?" Fluse asked incredulously.

"Schmidt is loyal, but not particularly bright. That's why we've had such an easy time dealing with them and their cars. Ritter is no fool, but he's surrounded by the dregs of Wegener's men."

"But he's still just another Wegener," Christian said. Schmidt had been a fool to follow Ritter. So why was Emil wasting time with him?

"Wegener was insane and fancied himself the next kaiser," Emil said. "Ritter is as sane as you or me. He sees a way to profit from the invasion, and he's smart enough to pull it off by keeping the aliens happy."

He stood up and paced the room. "We've got him trying to control the villages," he continued. "And if we believe him, there's at least one double agent of some kind on our team. We've also got gangs inside Paris that have developed an interest in our weapons, and broken supply lines that are bound to affect our capability to feed the civilians."

He stopped and made eye contact with Christian and the men, one by one. "Now, this might just be random chaos. It's only been a few months since the Martians resurfaced in the middle of a war. Or, it might all be connected."

"Connected?" Grundig said, wheezing.

"Why not?" Emil replied. "Ritter is smart. He looks like a peacock who seems more interested in his clothes than the military, but he's a trained soldier with an understanding of strategy. He knew I was playing Wegener the whole time I was in Reims, but Wegener wouldn't listen to him." He paused for a sip of coffee.

"So, trap us in Paris, cut off our supplies, and use the gangs to wear us down and steal our weapons," Christian said. "We need to eliminate Ritter and his men right away."

"Easier said than done," Fluse asked. "He's got the Martians backing him."

Emil nodded. "You're right. It's not time to go on the offensive."

Christian flushed with anger. They were going to sit around and wait? Still?

"But that doesn't mean we won't act like we're in a war again," Emil continued. "We need to establish access control to this compound. Put armed guards on the carts."

Christian relaxed a little. At least Emil understood the stakes now.

"We have a third Panzer ready, right?" Emil said, glancing at Grundig.

"Yes," Grundig replied, flashing his black teeth.

"And what about what Christian told us about the armor on that Wanderer he faced when he staged his latest mutiny?" Emil asked.

Christian winced at the dig.

"I'm almost done reworking the heat rays to put out more energy," Grundig said with a nod. "But his strategy of firing for their joints is still a great one."

"Excellent," Emil said. "Then it's time to make things official. Fluse, you're now our Panzer commander. We'll have to come up with a better term for that at some point."

Christian had to admit that Fluse had earned that responsibility. He had worked hard and come a long way. That had been especially evident during yesterday's skirmish.

"I want to think about how we can take advantage of having three armed and armored vehicles," Emil said. "Maybe two Panzers accompany all trips outside of this building, while one stays behind on guard. Decide how many men you need in your unit, who they should be, and so forth. And at some point, you're going to need to stay back here to manage guarding the compound, especially since we're going to have more heavy weapons for you, which takes me to my next decision."

Was Emil handing out assignments now? What did that mean? Why was Christian even there?

"Grundig, you're already doing a great job with weapons. Three Panzers will have to do for now. We need heat rays set up around the perimeter."

Christian agreed with this as well. Grundig had transformed himself from a potential liability to one of the most important men in the Marauders. He wouldn't have been interested in any kind of promotion, but giving him more authority over how the weapons were deployed made sense.

More than anything else, the Marauders were a team. They wore army uniforms. Even the French civilians tried to dress like they were part of an army, but that had more to do with the situation they found themselves in than any desire to be soldiers.

The Marauders were warriors; everyone here was part of the team. A team that, despite his feelings about how much more aggressive they should be, Christian wanted to be part of.

"Finally, Beckenbauer," Emil said.

Christian jumped at the use of his surname. It made whatever was coming sound more formal.

Was this it? Was Emil going to try to make him second-in-command again? Did Christian really want that?

"We've talked about this before," Emil continued as he stopped pacing, "and I want to discuss it now, with the other officers here. I apologize for putting you on the spot, but I need a way to delegate authority so I can oversee more of these operations."

He glanced away from Christian to look at the other men again. "I want to promote Beckenbauer to Leutnant and officially make him second-in-command, with a focus on running supply operations and reconnaissance on the ravageurs. This doesn't mean that he'll have direct authority over you two, but there will be times when I'm not around or too busy to get involved in day-to-day ops. When that happens, he'll be my voice. Do I hear any objections?"

Emil's eyes fell on Christian first. Christian looked down at his boots. They could have used a shine.

He *was* a soldier. The way he felt about the scuffs and marks on his footwear made him realize that. Soldiers sacrificed their feelings for the greater good. Soldiers were part of a team.

He nodded his acknowledgment to Emil, who smiled.

"Fluse, I know you were pretty upset with how he brought in Schmidt," Emil went on.

"I am," Fluse said. "But he came through for us yesterday. He showed amazing restraint during the riot, especially after we took that prisoner."

So Fluse had noticed that, and now he was speaking up for a member of his team. Christian blinked away a tear.

"Schmidt told me where Ritter is," Emil said. "Or at least where he was a few days ago."

Christian gasped at the same time Fluse did.

"But attacking him would be suicide," Emil added. "He's got at least fifty men, and he always has a Martian escort."

"How does he talk to them, I wonder?" Grundig said, stroking his chin.

"Actually, I want you to discuss that with Schmidt. They have some kind of machine that prints words in response to Ritter's questions."

"Fascinating," Grundig said, showing his black teeth again.

"We can't attack Ritter, but that doesn't mean we can't scout the area around him and learn more about what he's doing, who he's talking to, and what his real plans might be. That's what I want you to look into, Christian. I'll help you with the planning."

Finally, they were taking action.

"Stealth will be the name of the game here," Emil said, making direct eye contact with Christian. "And patience. Are we all agreed?"

Christian and the others nodded.

CHAPTER 12

THE MARAUDERS' HEADQUARTERS, PARIS FRANCE

Serpent didn't walk into the courtyard. He waddled, moving as if his hips and brain weren't on speaking terms. But he stood more than two meters tall, with massive arms and matching shoulders. But Christian wasn't ready to recommend he cut back on the wine and pastries. Not to his face, at least.

Christian opted not to remark on Serpent's grooming habits, either. His scraggly hair flowed down to his shoulders, his beard was an unkempt mess, and Christian could sense his stench from half a city block away. He was dressed more for a lazy morning at a local café than negotiations, with a shirt that barely covered his ample gut and still bore evidence of his breakfast. The only thing that marked him as a gang member was his red bandanna, the colors of the Maîtres Rouges.

And now Serpent was toddling outside the Marauders' headquarters like he owned the place. Based on the latest word about Paris's gang activity, he wasn't far from wrong. But regardless of how many arrondissements he controlled, the Marauders had something he wanted: one of his men.

Serpent, Christian had learned, led the gang that had tried to take the Marauders' heat ray two days earlier. The gang had shot up a neighborhood at the same time, risking countless lives over a squabble with a rival group. Serpent didn't deserve an audience with Emil, in Christian's opinion. The only thing he had coming was a rope around his neck and a rickety stool under his feet.

But killing Serpent would merely open a spot for another thug. This meeting was about showing him that the Marauders had nothing to fear from him, and that further attempts to steal from them would only lead to more trouble.

"Where is this leader?" Serpent said in French. "This Emil?"

"You will wait here," Fluse said.

"I don't wait for anyone," Serpent retorted.

"If you want to talk to Hauptmann Zimmerman, you will wait."

Serpent glowered at Fluse's back as Fluse turned to enter the headquarters. Christian stepped between them with his rifle in his hand and made eye contact with the gang leader.

This had all been planned in advance, of course. Emil had known exactly when Serpent would arrive and could have been waiting for the gang leader in the courtyard. But word on the street was that Serpent was a proud man.

Proud men didn't like to be kept waiting.

Serpent crossed his arms. Then he sniffed. Tapped a foot on the ground. Grunted. Checked his watch.

Christian smiled. Serpent sneered in response.

Finally, Emil strode out into the courtyard. His uniform shirt was unbuttoned, with one sleeve rolled to his elbow while the other hung loose around his wrist with an unfastened cuff. He was a man preparing for a nap, not someone waiting for an important visitor.

It was all part of the plan.

Emil had already understood a bit of French before the German Army had drafted him. He'd worked on the Planetary Warning System, which involved speaking to different countries. He'd also picked up a bit more French after the Marauders had arrived in Paris. But they'd decided that making Serpent speak through an interpreter would be even more humiliating.

"So, how can my commander help you?" Fluse asked.

"What do you mean?" Serpent growled, now speaking in thick German. "You know why I'm here."

"You want to *try* to speak German?" Fluse asked. "Okay."

"Try? I didn't have any trouble talking to the other—I mean, I can talk your language. Give me back my man."

Christian raised an eyebrow. Other? What other had the gang leader been talking about?

"We caught your man trying to steal one of our carts," Emil said. "Stealing a horse gets the noose these days, but you expect us to hand over a man who tried to take *two* horses, a cart, and one of our weapons?"

"You already killed my other man," Serpent said. "Left him lying in the street!"

Emil crossed his arms. "Like I said, horse thieves aren't treated kindly after this new Martian Attack. Do the Maîtres Rouges have rules stating that only one thief in two is punished?"

Serpent raised an arm over his head. The four men guarding him, including Christian, raised their rifles.

"You are a guest here," Fluse said in French. "Control yourself."

Serpent lowered his arms. "What do you want?" he asked, struggling to keep his voice even.

"I want you to tell me what you planned on doing with my heat ray," Emil said.

Serpent laughed. "What do you think I'd do with it? Wipe out my enemies. Take over this city!"

"And you just thought of this two days ago? We've been here for months, and you ignored us. And now you decide you're going to send two men against a squad of mine to steal a heat ray? Don't talk to me like I'm an idiot, Serpent. You'll only make me angry."

Serpent leaned back on one foot. "What are you saying?"

"Who are you working for?"

When Serpent had requested this meeting, Emil had raised to Christian the prospect of Ritter being involved. Word was that Serpent had been a smuggler and weapons dealer before the invasion, so the idea that he'd be working with someone outside the city made sense.

"Serpent works for no man!" the gang leader shouted.

"No *man*," Emil repeated. "So, the Martians then?"

"What?" Serpent raised his arms and stepped toward Emil. Christian trained his rifle directly on the gang leader's head, and the other three guards followed suit. Fluse shouted another warning in French.

Serpent took a big step back and held up his hands. "I would never work with those monstres," he said sullenly. "I am here to negotiate, not be insulted."

If Serpent was dealing with Ritter, he either didn't know who else was involved, or he was putting on an impressive show. So Christian wasn't surprised that Emil went in for the kill just then.

"Fine," Emil said, uncrossing his arms. "I wanted to be sure. There's at least one group of renegades—ravageurs—who are working with the aliens. You wouldn't leave here alive if we thought you were with them."

Serpent's brow wrinkled, but he said nothing.

"You can have your man back. He's of no use to me, and there's no reason for anyone else to die over failed plans." Emil gestured back to the building. "But understand this: we won't be taking prisoners from here on."

The door opened then, and two Marauders escorted Serpent's man outside.

"Is there anything else you'd like to discuss?" Emil asked with a broad smile. "Do you need some food or water for your men?"

"I can take care of my own!" Serpent said, scowling. But the look of confusion returned as he and his man were guided out of the courtyard.

"That was certainly interesting," Emil said as he poured himself a cup of coffee from the urn in the mess hall.

"Did you hear him catch himself?" Christian asked. "When he said he'd spoken to some other? Do you think he meant Ritter?"

"Almost certainly."

"Then what do we do?" Fluse asked.

Emil sat down at one of the tables. "Keep an eye on him. There's nothing else we can do for now. A battle with his gang would destroy most of this city and do Ritter's work for him. But if he really is working with Serpent, they're going to have a serious talk soon."

"Ritter creates chaos for us," Fluse said. "So now we create chaos for him."

"Yes," Emil said. "An ugly game, but better than one fought with bullets and heat rays."

CHAPTER 13

AUGUST 1900: LEIMERSHEIM, GERMANY

Inside his family's barn, Christian rolled the knife in his palm, testing its weight and feeling the smooth, polished sides of the fine rosewood. It was a gift from Opa for his eleventh birthday, a handmade folding model with polished grips and German stainless steel.

He unfolded it, snapping the handle as if the knife had a spring to open the blade, and cut the strings holding the bale of hay together. They exploded open with a satisfying *pop* after the slightest touch of his blade. Christian smiled as he folded the blade back into the grip with the skill of a boy who had practiced the move a thousand times before.

He took an armful of hay to the first stall where Hans, the clever old draft horse, impatiently stamped his hoof.

"Here you go," Christian whispered as he filled the trough. "Sorry I'm so—"

A throbbing hum interrupted Christian before he could finish. The sound resonated in his stomach, like when he sat too close to the organ at church.

A woman's scream was cut off. Was that Mother?

Christian dropped the remains of the hay and ran out of the barn—and into chaos.

The house was engulfed in flames. Father was running toward it from the other direction, where he'd been working in the fields. The chickens had fled their coop and were running in circles.

But Christian's eyes were drawn beyond the pandemonium and the burning house to a water tower that hadn't been there before. It stood just past the house, teetering on three steel legs. When did it get there? Who'd built it?

And then the water tower moved, stepping closer to the barn on its snaky, spindly legs and raising a thin metallic arm to point something in Christian's direction. The deep hum rose again, so loud this time that his teeth vibrated and hurt.

Something hurled him to the ground. After a moment, Christian realized that Opa was lying over him. The humming had ceased, replaced by the scream of horses.

The barn was burning. The horses inside abruptly stopped screaming.

Christian tried to right himself, pushing his hands against the ground, but Opa scooped him up.

"This way!" Opa said, carrying Christian under one arm like a bag of flour. He stopped in the center of the farmyard, looking in one direction and then the other. The walking water tower's arm turned toward them, and Opa ran again, this time toward the well.

"You'll be safe from these bastards here, Christian," Opa said. "Remember us."

And then Christian fell, landing hard inside the well. He nearly passed out from the shock of the cold water, but he regained his senses after a few seconds.

"Opa? Hello? Opa? Father? Help!"

The hum rose again, echoing off the stone sides of the well. Screams drowned out Christian's cries for help. Some of those screams came from the horses that had been out to pasture, but at least one of them sounded like a man.

Then the humming stopped. Silence hung over the farm like a dense winter fog.

Christian called for help until his throat was sore. He pounded on the walls of the well, slapped the water in fear and desperation. Nobody answered. He drank from the well to soothe his throat, then shouted some more.

But the silence soaked up his screams.

After a while, his arms and legs became sore. Christian paddled around the well and found a tiny ledge where, if he was careful, he could take short rests.

The sun set.

The sun rose.

Keeping his head above water became Christian's entire life. The sun set and rose at least one more time as the screams and gut-wrenching hums echoed in his memories, but the shock of cold water on his face kept bringing him back to the present.

Eventually, voices sounded from above. Christian dunked under the water to wake himself up. The voices were still there when he resurfaced.

"Help! Help!" Christian screamed so hard that he stopped paddled and submerged himself again. He choked on the freezing water, heaved it up, then bellowed, "Help me! I'm down here!"

A man's head appeared at the top of the well, then another. Within a few minutes, Christian was climbing up a rope. His cold muscles screamed in protest, but nothing was going to stop him from getting out of that hole in the ground.

Three men met him at the top of the well. Two of them were soldiers, and the other was a priest.

Christian noticed then that his home and the barn were piles of ash. Deep down, he'd already known his family was gone, but he scanned the farm anyway. He spotted a much smaller pile of black ash near the house, but the priest grabbed him and turned him away from it.

"Get me a blanket!" the priest said. "This boy is freezing!"

"Where are my parents?" Christian asked. "Where's my grandfather?"

His rescuers looked at each other before the priest answered, "We'll take you to Karlsruhe. If your parents are still . . . around, they'll find you there."

As they walked to the soldier's cart, Christian spotted his knife on the ground. He reached down and picked it up.

"That's not a toy," the priest barked. "Give me that." He grabbed it and tucked it into his pocket.

Christian never saw that last tie to his previous life again.

CHAPTER 14

SEPTEMBER 1915: THE ROAD TO GOUSSAINVILLE, FRANCE

The leaves were starting to turn, framing the road in gorgeous browns, yellows, and reds. Flocks of birds were flying south overhead, oblivious to the struggles of villagers, marauders, ravageurs, and aliens below. Christian wondered whether the world would have been better off if the war ended with nobody left.

The Renault rumbled ahead, close enough that the rattle of its tracks was audible but far enough away that it didn't drown out the more consequential business of the migrating geese. The new German Panzer, a model Christian wasn't familiar with, rumbled far behind the two carts that followed Christian's. They didn't have three carts worth of supplies, of course, but Christian desperately hoped that they might have three carts of crops to ferry back to Paris for distribution to the southern villages with damaged or fallow fields.

Another rumbling wound its way into Christian's consciousness. It was too high-pitched to be a Panzer, and too mechanical to be a bird or an insect. A car, maybe?

He scanned the horizon. A small blotch of black and gray was speeding from left to right.

Christian held his right hand up in a fist, the signal to stop.

The other two cart drivers imitated him, and the convoy slowed to a halt. He picked up his M98, eager to test the scope Grundig had made for him.

It was a car sporting makeshift armor.

Miller, Fluse's newly minted deputy and the Panzer commander on this mission, climbed up onto Christian's cart. "I see it," he said. "We can catch it in the Renault. Only need to get within a few hundred meters to destroy it."

Christian agreed that they probably could. But what then? His best guess was that Ritter's headquarters was only a dozen or so kilometers to the west, and destroying one of his cars so nearby might make him want to move. That would ruin the Marauders' longer-term strategy.

Emil's orders had been clear: Keep a low profile. Get the supplies to the villages, and bring back whatever you can. And, do not engage unless attacked.

"You're probably right," Christian said, nodding. "But that's not our job. Not yet."

"Why not? It's one car!" Miller ran his fingers through his thick blond hair. "It's alone. Anything we can take away from them is a win for us."

Miller wasn't entirely wrong. The Renault would take the other vehicle out before it had fired a single shot in defense, and it might take days for Ritter to figure out what had happened. They could even burn the car down to slag and make it that much harder to find.

But before Christian could respond, Miller shifted to jump off the cart, saying, "I'll drive the Panzer."

"What?" Christian said, the motion knocking him out of his reverie. "No. I said *no*. Our orders from Hauptmann Zimmerman are to not engage. Our best outcome is for them to never learn that we were here."

"Don't give me orders. I'm the Panzer commander here."

"I *am* giving you orders. Don't make me pull rank, Miller. You know we're not supposed to be hunting today. If you pursue that car, you'd be violating Emil's orders, not just mine."

"Oh, so countermanding orders only works for you?"

It was a cheap shot, but typical of Miller. He'd been another sparring partner of Emil's back at the Somme and nearly as unpopular as Fluse. But like his assertion about the car, his jab wasn't entirely wrong. Christian was literally ordering Miller to not do what he'd done in the past.

"Let's just wait for it to pass and deliver the supplies like we were told," Christian said. "Please?"

Miller stood on the cart and set his jaw. "You wasted too much time anyway. Signal when you're ready to go again." Then he stomped back to the Panzer in the rear of the convoy.

Louis had his market tables arranged when the convoy arrived in Goussainville. The villagers had a generous assortment of fruit, cured pork, and even a few loaves of baked bread. Christian brought his cart to a halt near the tables, and the other two carts lined up behind him. Miller brought the Panzer to a halt and exited from the back with his gunner. He scowled at Christian before walking away.

Fine. Let Miller sulk. If he didn't come around later, Christian would have a talk with Fluse about it.

The Marauders met the residents with laughs, handshakes, and hugs. Then both groups got to work unloading the cart and filling up what appeared to be a little more than two cartloads to take home.

Goussainville was a home away from home, if Christian even still thought of Leimersheim as home. He'd finished school and played football there, but the church had always made sure he never felt like he belonged. Sometimes he caught himself daydreaming about retiring to a village like Goussainville when this war ended.

Assuming it ended with humans having homes at all.

The work was done in short order, giving the Marauders plenty of time to rest before the return trip to Paris. Louis brought out a few more loaves of bread, some cheese, and a bottle of wine for them to eat.

Happy shouts and the tapping of small feet reverberated across the village street, pulling Christian's attention back to the present and in the direction of the shared well that served as the centerpiece of the village square. The little girl who had startled Christian a few weeks earlier was back, dancing on the edge of the well again, while a younger boy ran in circles on the ground around her. The girl stopped, looked at Christian, and said something to him in French.

"Pardon?" Christian said, approaching her to hear her better.

She repeated herself, and Christian worked out that she was asking him where he was from. He really needed to talk to Fluse about more French lessons.

"Uh, Allemagne," Christian said.

"Merci de nous aider," she said.

Christian tilted his head. He only understood that she was thanking him for something. "Pardon?"

"She is thanking you for helping us, Herr Beckenbauer," a voice said from behind him.

Christian spun around and saw Louis, who added, "And I thank you, too. I don't know what would have become of us without you Maraudeurs. Clearly, you were sent by God."

"Well, uh, thank you," Christian said, his voice heavy with emotion.

"You have family back home?" Louis asked. "Do you know what happened to them?"

"Um . . . no."

Louis placed a hand on Christian's shoulder. "I am sorry. I should mind my own business."

Christian swallowed and wiped a tear. "No. It's fine, Louis. Thank you for asking."

The little girl laughed and began chasing the boy around the well.

CHAPTER 15

SOMEWHERE NORTHWEST OF PARIS, FRANCE

Ritter and his men were making no effort to conceal themselves. Four towering Wanderers encircled their camp, and the smoke of their wood fires was noticeable from the hilltop Christian and Otto were camping on more than a kilometer away.

The irrational urge to open fire on the Wanderers came to the surface again for Christian. But he and Otto were alone, with no Panzers or carts. This was a low-profile scouting mission, intended to verify that Schmidt had been telling Emil the truth and gather an assessment of how well-outfitted Ritter was.

"What do they have?" Otto asked, pen in hand. Hopefully, someone would be able to decipher his left-handed, apelike scrawl for Christian back at Marauders' headquarters.

"Four Wanderers, at least fifty men, eight armored cars, and ten horses," Christian said as he lowered the field glasses. "They're set up in a flat spot that's partially encircled by some trees and a heavy thicket. They've built temporary guard shelters at what they're using for an entrance, and they've got two guards on the perimeter. Here. Take a look."

Otto whistled quietly as he peered through the binoculars. "Four Wanderers?"

"Posted at the corners," Christian answered. "They'd make great guard towers, but Martians rely on hearing, not sight. Are they letting guards into those things? Or do the aliens listen and blast their horns when they sense something?"

"Where are they getting their food from?" Otto said. "That reminds me. Did I tell you about this thing Charlotte baked me? Quiche, I think? It's like a pie made from eggs! Her father has a bunch of chickens . . ."

Christian checked his watch. Fifteen minutes between references to Charlotte. Otto must have been tired, but he had a point. How was Ritter restocking? Both of the nearby villages had looked destitute when Christian and Otto had passed near them. They'd need to risk showing their faces to find out for sure. But if Ritter had contacts in the towns, he'd get word of two strangers asking questions.

"Let's set up camp here," Christian suggested, interrupting Otto. "They don't have anyone with a scope or field glasses who's keeping watch, so we're pretty much invisible here if we don't start a fire. Set up your tent, and I'll wake you after sunset."

The dim light of a new moon would make it easier for Christian and Otto to move closer to Ritter's camp without being seen. However, the Wanderers meant that they still needed to be careful about making noise.

So Christian decided that the best tactic was circling the camp from the east and approaching from the back, where the thicket would absorb any sound they made as they worked their way toward the enemy. From there, they could enter the camp and learn what they could about Ritter's camp and his plans.

Whenever the going got tough, Otto would lose his farm boy demeanor and transform into one of the Marauders' most reliable soldiers. That was why Christian had chosen to bring him instead of Miller, who'd campaigned hard to come along. He was arguably a better soldier than Otto, but his zeal made Christian a little nervous. Not to mention Fluse wanted Miller to run the Panzers for the supply convoys anyway.

Christian checked the time when he and Otto reached the back of the camp, which was still a few hundred meters from the thicket. It was 00:30. The two of them hunkered down and waited.

Just then, an earsplitting blast from a Wanderer cut through the night. Christian threw himself to the ground, covering his ears. The clanking of articulated legs sounded from the camp, and two Wanderers strode out.

Had they heard Christian and Otto? Christian held his breath and waited.

The Wanderers approached the two men, then abruptly turned and headed northeast as two more Wanderers emerged from the night and strode past them.

"Shift change?" Otto whispered.

Christian lay there silently until he heard quiet voices approaching from the direction of the camp. Guards. He'd seen patrols walking the perimeter in opposite directions before he and Otto had left the hill.

Ritter's men were lackadaisical, crossing at both the front and back of the camp. This would give Otto and Christian plenty of time to approach the thicket and try to enter the camp without alerting the Martians.

Two guards approached from either direction, stopping almost directly in front of where Otto and Christian were lying prone in the tall grass.

"Seen anything?" one of the guards asked.

"What do you think?"

"Owls? Grass? Bats?"

The first guard snickered, and the other one chuckled. One of them struck a match, and they lit their cigarettes.

All Christian had to do was ready his rifle, aim at one of the men, and fire. There was plenty of time to drop all four of them.

But that would alert the Martians and upend the Marauders' plans.

The guards moved on and quickly fell out of sight.

"That's some poor discipline," Otto said. "Emil would be furious if they were his men."

Christian stifled a laugh as he remembered the Emil Zimmerman he'd met in the trenches of the Somme—the one who'd nearly been court-martialed for assaulting Leutnant Fluse.

After ensuring the guards were well out of sight, Christian and Otto proceeded toward the thicket. Hopefully, any noise they made would be confused with the footsteps of the guards. Those men weren't even trying to be quiet.

The wall of trees, bramble, and ivy that ringed this part of Ritter's compound was thick enough to completely conceal the camp. It had obviously been placed there by a human—or at least cultivated to act as a natural pen for livestock or some sort of assembly area. Still, Christian carefully edged his way in, trying to make as little noise as possible. The Martians had demonstrated uncanny hearing in the past.

He made his way in for a few meters before he could finally make out a campfire and the outline of the line of cars he'd seen from the hill. Shadows danced back and forth in front of him, magnified by the distance between their subjects and the light from the campfire.

Christian gestured for Otto to wait, then slipped into a narrow gap in the dense foliage. He emerged into a tiny opening where the light from the fire was considerably brighter. The sweet perfume of Benzin blended with the sharp bite of the pine smoke.

The armored cars were visible now, as were a cluster of men relaxing with bottles of beer on the fender of a Mercedes at one end of the makeshift motor pool.

It was 01:00, and Ritter's men were drinking? Maybe he ran

shifts, and this group had a day off? Or, maybe working with aliens meant military discipline was no longer necessary.

Christian hunkered down and strained to eavesdrop on their conversation.

". . . So I had to burn their barn down," one soldier finished saying.

"Well, they need to wise up," another soldier said before taking a swig of beer. "Like the boss said, times are changing."

"Not fast enough," said a third soldier. "We've been stuck out here for weeks. When do we move to the city?"

"What are you complaining about?" asked the second soldier. "You're sitting here with good beer. Your stomach is full from a better meal than we ever got in Reims."

"Yeah, the boss takes care of us," echoed a fourth soldier. "Stop your complaining. We're going to start taking the villages soon, just you wait. Then we'll work our way to Paris and take out those traitors who ruined Reims."

Traitors! The same word Schmidt had used. Christian clenched his teeth. Ritter was planning on taking Paris. That wasn't much of a surprise, but hearing the men say it out loud made his blood boil.

He had two full clips on him. He could probably play sniper for a long time before any of these soldiers found him in the dark—

No. That wasn't the plan. That was his thirst for revenge talking.

A scraping noise brought Christian back to the present. Otto was directly behind him, trying to fit into the tiny clearing.

"What was that?" said one of the men by the Mercedes.

Christian glowered at Otto, holding his finger over his lips. Otto stared back at him, frozen in place.

A light shined toward them, scanning back and forth over the thicket. "Relax, Heinz!" said one soldier. "It's probably just a raccoon."

The other soldiers chuckled derisively.

Christian waited silently with Otto for the soldiers to finish their beers. He had hoped to find the machine Ritter was using to talk to the Martians, but Otto's blunder had ruined those plans. So once the soldiers had disappeared, the two of them slowly backed out of the clearing and worked their way back to camp.

CHAPTER 16
PARIS, FRANCE

The Eiffel Tower had dominated the Paris skyline since it had been erected, but never more so than after the second Martian Attack. The aliens had leveled nearly every structure taller than three stories in the city, including the Arc de Triomphe. Only the tower and Notre-Dame had been spared. Now, the top of the Eiffel Tower loomed on the horizon as Christian rode on horseback with Otto past the fetid ruins of the wholesale meat markets on the northeastern edge of the city. They'd ridden hard since leaving their camp near Ritter's headquarters early in the morning, and Christian was looking forward to dinner, shower, and a good night's sleep

"I'll never get used to that stench," Otto said.

Christian nodded in agreement.

"Wait," Otto said, pointing toward the south. "Is that smoke?"

It was. A black plume was rising into the darkening sky.

"Yes, it's fire," Christian said before urging his horse onward. Any fire in a city as dense as Paris was a disaster. Christian didn't need to be amid the carnage caused by the aliens and their heat rays to remember that.

Soon, the sounds of gunfire were audible over the galloping of their horses. Christian tugged on the reins and guided his horse into an alley before bringing them to a stop. "It's another riot," he said when Otto pulled up next to him.

Otto grimaced.

"We need to get this intelligence back to headquarters," Christian said. "You go ahead and make sure Emil gets your notes and that map. I'll see if he's sent anyone out to end this mess yet."

He dismounted and threw the saddlebag that held his ammunition over his shoulder. The sound of gunfire was growing more intense. "You might want to tie up your horse here and walk," he added. "Otherwise, you're a moving target."

"Are you sure?" asked Otto, raising his voice over the din.

"Sure about what?" Christian asked.

"That you want to go into that mess alone?"

"It's not going to be much easier for you to make it back to headquarters. But if we're both killed out here, we wasted three days and Emil will have to send someone else."

"Okay. I'll ride back a bit and try to circle the fighting." Otto then rode off with his horse in the direction he and Christian had come from.

Christian made sure his mount was secure, then chambered a round and walked down the city street, hugging the wall. The next alley was engulfed in smoke from a burning barrel, and the staccato of small weapons fire filled his ears.

He reached another corner and craned his neck around to see. It was a full-on firefight. On one side of the street, men wearing the red bandannas of the Maîtres were firing at the men in black watch caps who occupied the other side.

Were the Maîtres Rouges Christian's enemy? And was the other gang automatically the Marauders' allies? Charging into this conflagration had seemed like a good idea a few minutes ago, but what could Christian really do?

Look for civilians in trouble and shepherd them away from the violence. Save lives instead of taking them. Yes, that was what Christian could do.

He braced himself. But before he could turn the corner, the clatter of hoofs and the scream of a horse rose from the direction he'd come in.

Otto?

Christian ran back that way, heedless of any danger. He flew past the alley where he and Otto had separated and made it a few hundred more yards before a group of men surrounding a fallen horse was visible.

One of the men was kicking something. The horse?

No, he was kicking another man. Otto.

Otto struggled to one knee and held up a hand. The man kicked him in the face, knocking him back to the ground.

Christian brought his M98 up. The men were near, and the scope made aiming difficult, but he squeezed off a round and took down the man kicking Otto with a shot in the head. He shifted the scope to the right and fired again. A little lower this time, getting his next target in the neck.

The other three froze, then took off running.

Christian squeezed the trigger again. Got the third man in the back.

He breathed the way the range sergeant had taught him. It let him still himself when the desire for revenge threatened to overtake him.

He exhaled, then squeezed the trigger again. Got the fourth man in the back of the head.

Again he breathed, then squeezed the trigger. The last man was down.

Christian ran to Otto as he pulled a clip out of the saddlebag and fed it into the M98. Otto's face was a mangled mess, and he was missing teeth. He tried to stand again but fell back onto the street. The front of his uniform was soaked with blood. He was bleeding out.

"Stay with me, Otto!" Christian said as he rushed to his comrade's side. "I have you."

"I . . . I . . . Charlotte," Otto said.

"It's okay. You'll see her soon. I'll get my horse and get you home to the medic."

The breath rattled in Otto's chest, and he closed his eyes.

He was gone.

Christian stood up. His heart raced as heat rose in his face. The street was still, with only the sound of shots echoing from where he'd run from disturbing a deceptively quiet neighborhood.

That was when Christian remembered Otto's notes.

He bent down over Otto and checked his pack. The notes were right on top. Christian shoved them into the saddlebag, taking his last five clips out and distributing them in his uniform pockets.

He stood again, then took off toward the sound of gunfire at a full sprint. He shouldered his rifle when he reached the corner and found his first target, a man wearing a red bandanna.

The clip was empty in a few seconds, and five Maîtres were down.

Christian withdrew long enough to reload.

He targeted the black watch caps this time. Took four down, and missed one.

They knew he was there now. Shots struck the corner of the building as Christian reloaded. One penetrated the soft wood and nicked him in his shoulder. He dropped to the ground and peered around. The gangs had lost interest and started shooting at each other again.

Christian exhaled, then squeezed the trigger. A Maître this time. He'd put the round in the man's shoulder so that it wouldn't be clear where the shot had come from.

Again he exhaled, then squeezed the trigger. Two black watch caps were taken down with a single shot. He hadn't been trying for that.

Once more, faster this time. A third black watch cap. The last in their group was alone until a Maître took him down while he stared at his dead comrades.

The Maîtres stood and cheered. Idiots. Six of them, in fact.

Christian shot two, then reloaded without stopping to take cover. The survivors faced him and opened fire in panic. But panicked men often couldn't hit their targets.

With four shots, Christian took the last four men down.

A Panzer rolled up from the direction where Christian had been shooting. It stopped, and the back door opened and four men, with Miller in the lead, stepped out holding M98s.

Christian waited. When no shots were fired at the Panzer, he stood up and waved his hand. Then he slowly walked toward the black watch cap position to make sure he'd left no survivors.

"Beckenbauer!" Miller shouted as he approached Christian, looking back and forth to survey the area. "What happened here?"

"Some kind of riot. Otto and I rode right into it." Christian crossed his arms. "They . . . they got him."

"Bumpkin?" Miller said, his eyes wide. "He's down? Are you okay?"

Christian pointed down the street. "He's over there. They pulled him right off his horse."

"Who pulled him? Where's your horse?"

"Tied up. Otto was trying to ride around this to make sure our intelligence from Ritter's camp made it to Emil. I came here to see what was happening and then heard them attack him. So I went back . . ." Christian's voice trailed off then.

"You went back to help him?" Miller asked. "Then what?" By then, Fluse had stepped out from behind the Panzer and joined them.

Christian looked at Miller and Fluse. He didn't want to talk anymore.

"Your horse is still there?" Miller went on. "You were afraid they'd get you if you tried to ride? You waited here until they all killed each other?"

"I wasn't afraid," Christian answered finally. "And they didn't kill each other."

CHAPTER 17

THE TWELFTH ARRONDISSEMENT, PARIS, FRANCE

"We needed this," said Fluse, holding up his hands to indicate the light rain.

"You were a farmer?" Christian asked as they rode toward the quartier de Picpus, a neighborhood that had housed many factory workers before the invasion.

"Oh no, not at all," Fluse said, pointing to himself. "I'm a city boy. But I heard that saying often enough that it comes automatically."

It was a valiant attempt to cheer Christian up. Plus, Fluse had a point. It had been a dry past few weeks; and even here, in a mostly urban neighborhood, the earthy scent of petrichor took Christian's mind off where he was and what he was doing.

When he let it, of course.

They were riding to Picpus to find Charlotte's tenement. Her name had literally been the last word on Otto's lips when he'd passed, so letting her know what had happened was the least that Christian could do.

He and Fluse had a map that one of Madame Curie's men had drawn, and they were following it down a street that led to row after row of identical buildings. They were utilitarian structures, indistinguishable from one another; and after only a few blocks, the map was their only tether to the outside world.

They reached a corner manned by men wearing blue bandannas on their right arms—another of the many gangs that roamed Paris. Christian's right hand subconsciously reached toward the inside breast pocket of his jacket, but he caught it before drawing attention to the pistol hidden there.

The tallest of the men stepped forward and spoke in rapid-fire French. Fluse answered, and the man waved them on.

"What did you say?" Christian asked.

"The truth," Fluse said. "This group is friendly with the Resistance."

"Where did you learn French?" Christian asked. Fluse's knowledge of the language had proven invaluable to the Marauders, and it had just occurred to Christian that he didn't know why the Leutnant knew it so well.

"My father was stationed on the border for a few years before I was born," Fluse said wistfully. "Sometimes he spoke French to us. Said that we should learn how to expand our view of the world. Only now do I understand what he meant. I took French in university because it was an easy class."

"Your father was military, too?"

"Yes. Killed during the first Martian Attack."

Everyone had lost someone to the aliens, either directly or because of the chaos they'd sewn. Christian gritted his teeth.

This neighborhood had survived the latest Martian Attack unscathed, but it was only another of the aliens' cruel jokes: Much of the industrial zones near the Seine had been all but destroyed. The people had survived, but their livelihoods and food supply had not. Most had left this part of the city, hoping to find a better situation elsewhere.

"Here it is," said Fluse. They were stopped in front of number forty-two on rue Neuvième.

They tied their horses to the fence in front of the building and rang the bell for apartment number six. The door made a strange buzzing noise.

"What the hell was that?" Christian asked, jumping back.

Fluse shrugged. "Maybe the attack damaged the electrical grid here?"

The door buzzed again. Was it electric? Would it shock Christian if he touched it?

He stared at Fluse, who was staring back at him. Both of them were afraid of moving, it seemed.

Finally, the door opened, and a shockingly beautiful face studied them. "Bonjour?"

"Charlotte?" asked Fluse.

"Oui?"

Fluse said something to her, quickly at first, and then his words slowed. Christian could comprehend Otto's name and the word *mort*.

Charlotte stood stock-still for a moment, one hand holding the door open, the other bracing her on its frame. She was the most beautiful woman Christian had ever seen, with long black hair, the prophesied tiny button nose, and deep blue eyes.

After a long ten seconds, she finally spoke again.

"She's invited us in," Fluse said.

"I don't think I want to—" Christian began.

"We really should." Fluse gently guided Christian toward the door with his hand.

Christian turned to check the horses. Again, Fluse pushed him toward Charlotte, and she led them inside. Christian could probably find his way back to headquarters, even without the map. But Fluse wasn't giving him a choice.

The hallway was dark, even with the electric lights, and longer than Christian had imagined. The buildings were deep, with eight units on each floor. Charlotte lived all the way in the back.

"She says the doors have electric locks," Fluse explained. "That noise meant she was unlocking the door so we could push our way in. She's expecting a friend for coffee today, and she thought they were early."

Christian nodded. This was another of the innovations the Curies had made possible after the first Martian Attack. Their modern technology was outliving the city.

Charlotte led them in through her apartment door, quietly speaking the entire time. They crossed a small living room with a well-worn sofa against one wall and a bookcase on the other. A little girl sat on the sofa. She must have been eight or nine years old, with the same perfect hair and button nose as Charlotte; and when she looked up from her picture book, her eyes—which were also the same as Charlotte's—seemed to pierce Christian in place.

Charlotte spoke to the girl in French, and the girl replied.

"This is Patty, Charlotte's daughter," Fluse said.

Otto had mentioned Patty a few times. But Christian had imagined she was a sister or a niece, not Charlotte's daughter.

"Hello, Patty," said Christian.

The girl smiled and went back to her book.

Charlotte led Christian and Fluse to the kitchen and gestured toward the table. Her hands were clean, with perfectly manicured nails. How did she keep them so nice while working at a laundry?

"Her father is out today, visiting family," Fluse translated again.

The table faced a large picture window with a view of a shared yard. The chickens that had supplied their unborn offspring for Otto's quiche were huddled in a small coop.

Charlotte poured coffee for Christian and Fluse, then put out bread and cheese.

"She doesn't have to feed us," Christian said.

"She wants to," Fluse said. "And if I can be so bold, a Sunday afternoon away from the Marauders might do you some good, Christian."

"We're here to tell her that her boyfriend was killed, and she's going to comfort me?"

The only response from Fluse was a stony look.

Finally, after setting the table with jam, butter, and cream for the coffee, Charlotte sat down. "Your name is Christian?" she asked in halting German.

"Yes," Christian replied.

The coffee was strong, as if it had been sitting on the cast-iron stove since early that morning. Christian added extra cream to it.

"And you are Gerhard?" she asked Fluse.

"Yes."

"Otto mention you," she said. "Good friends."

"You understand some German?" Fluse asked.

"Only a little."

"How did you meet Otto?"

"Ah," she said with a giggle, and continued in French.

"They met at a bakery," Fluse translated. "Remember that time Otto brought home a dozen loaves of bread, and the cook nearly killed him? He bought them to impress her!" Fluse laughed at that.

Charlotte laughed with him, then continued with a question.

"It seems she's a shrewd judge of character, Christian," Fluse said. "She already figured out you were there when it happened. She wants to hear your story."

"No."

"S't plait," Charlotte said, her blue eyes flaring. "Please."

Christian set his jaw, but he realized he couldn't say no again.

So he told the story, slowly at first, starting with the ride home from the north, assuming that no good would come of telling her about where he and Otto had been and why. Charlotte asked about the villages they had ridden through. It turned out that her family's farm had been close to Ritter's camp. Many families had fled that area because of the Martian activity during the new invasion.

Christian continued, describing the gang activity he and Otto had found when they'd entered Paris, and how they'd separated at the alley so that Otto could take their intelligence back to headquarters.

"Maîtres Rouges," Charlotte spat out when Christian described the gunfight he'd witnessed. Then she unleashed a flurry of French.

"What you two ran into happens somewhere every day," Fluse translated.

Christian went on, describing the scene he'd found when he'd run back to Otto. He stopped, trying to figure out how to finish his story without too much detail. Only then did he realize he was crying.

"Christian?" Charlotte asked.

"Sorry," Christian said, wiping his eyes with his sleeve.

He'd let Otto take those papers and ride into trouble. He hadn't ordered him to, but Christian had let him because he'd assumed he was taking the greater risk by heading toward the fighting.

He'd been wrong, and Otto was beaten like a dog in the street.

So Christian had killed those men.

Was he crying for Otto? Or for the men he'd shot? Had they even been wearing gang colors? He couldn't remember anymore.

Christian had killed men before. He'd been drafted without a choice into the kaiser's army, trained to kill, and sent to the front. Before the Martians had arrived on the Somme, it had been kill or be killed.

Only the most violent, twisted men enjoyed that. Was he one of them now?

Christian had only killed men in uniform and on the battle-field. Even the ravageurs were soldiers in an enemy army of sorts. But he'd never killed civilians in their own city, or shot someone as they fled.

Fluse spoke to Charlotte in French again. He knew the rest of the story, including Otto's last words.

Tears welled in Charlotte's eyes when she responded in French.

"The Martians killed her mother and husband when they drove her and her father off their farm," Fluse translated. "They fled here, hoping for food and shelter. They took this abandoned apartment and found work in the few places that were still open." His voice started to crack then. "They thought they were safe here because there were no Martians in Paris. At least not yet. But it's not safe, because of the people."

Patty entered the kitchen with her arms full. She emptied them onto the kitchen chair next to Christian and spoke to her mother.

"She wants to show us her toys," Fluse said.

Charlotte addressed her daughter reproachfully. But Christian wiped his eyes and nodded to Patty. "Tell Charlotte it's fine," he said. "I'd love to see what she has."

It was an assortment of toy soldiers carved from wood. On top of the pile was a cork from a wine or beer barrel with toothpicks sticking out of one end. Patty put the cork on the table so that it balanced on the tiny sticks.

The sticks were legs. It was a Wanderer.

Patty surrounded it with the soldiers and made shooting noises, as if they were fighting the Martian craft. She smiled at Christian before she asked him a question in French.

"She wants to know if you feel better," Fluse said, struggling to keep his voice even.

Christian nodded, then wiped his eyes before the new tears were visible. Patty had lost her grandmother and her father to the Martians.

"It is all she talks about," Charlotte said in French, with Fluse translating. "Fighting the Martians. She wants to be a Marauder."

Another child. Another attack. Another life lived for revenge. *And what happens when you run out of eyes?*

Christian and Fluse thanked Patty for her show, and Charlotte gave her a glass of milk before herding her back into the kitchen.

"Where will you go?" Christian asked when Charlotte returned. He dabbed at his eyes with a napkin.

"Oú? Where? We stay here. My father has friends. I have the laundry. There is a school here. There is . . ." She trailed off, then finished in French.

"She has nowhere to run, and fleeing won't help," Fluse translated. "Gangs. Martians. This is how we live now."

"So . . . you give up?" Christian blurted out before he could stop himself. "You surrender?"

Charlotte appeared confused for a moment, then smiled ruefully and spoke to Fluse.

"Acceptance and surrender are not the same thing," Fluse translated. "She can't go back and save her mother or tell her father to find a farm that the Martians won't destroy. She says she's not strong enough to stop that animal Serpent, and even if she was, another would take his place. She has what she has. This is where she is right now."

Charlotte took a sip of coffee before continuing in her rough German. "This coffee is . . . bitter. I can drink and be happy that I still have coffee. I can add cream and sugar to make it less. I can use it on the plants and make a fresh pot. Those are my choices. Or, I can drink it as it is and complain. That would be surrender."

"Otto found himself a very special woman," Fluse said.

Charlotte blushed as she looked down at her cup, then back to Christian with her beautiful eyes. "Do you need to leave?" she asked. "Or should I make another pot?"

Christian had come here with Fluse to tell her about Otto. To comfort her. To assure her that her friend had died a hero. He had wanted to tell her that Otto would be avenged. But more death was the last thing Charlotte wanted to hear about. She wasn't interested in revenge.

He nodded, and made himself a slice of bread with cheese.

CHAPTER 18

PARIS, FRANCE

The sun sat high in the sky, warming the cobblestones and making the unseasonably hot day more oppressive. Only an important conversation with Berlin over the wireless brought the Marauders out of the shade and onto the dangerous Paris streets. They marched in five ranks of two, weapons out with a round in the chamber. Paris didn't feel as safe as it had a week ago, before the Marauders had lost Otto.

"So you believe they'll send help our way?" Schmidt asked, hobbling along on his crutches.

To Christian, it was good hearing Schmidt say "we" instead of "you." Emil had been right about his former sergeant joining their cause. They'd spoken to Berlin and finally convinced Central Command to at least consider helping to defend Paris and take out Ritter.

"Sounds like it," Emil said. "They've got problems of their own, but they understand that protecting unoccupied cities like Paris benefits all of Europe. Even if they can't send troops, ammunition and other supplies would be spectacular."

"And they didn't know about Ritter," Schmidt said.

"No, they didn't. What you told them is what changed their

minds. You've done both your homeland and us a great service. Thank you."

"I had no idea Germany still had a government, let alone an Army. Ritter made it sound like the country had been destroyed." Schmidt shook his head. "I hope I can make up for trusting him."

Emil smiled as he placed a hand on Schmidt's shoulder. "You already have."

Less than a second later, Emil was lying on the ground, holding his own shoulder and groaning in pain.

The Marauders launched into action. Christian and Fluse carried Emil into a nearby recessed doorway as two more shots flew by, one throwing up a cloud of dust millimeters from Christian's left boot. Two more men dropped to the ground while pointing toward the second floor of a nearby building, while others returned fire.

"Miller!" Fluse shouted, pointing to the building where the shot had come from. "There!"

Miller waved to four of the Marauders. Together, they ran in a crouch toward the building, a bakery with apartments upstairs. He sent two soldiers to the back of the bakery, then heaved himself through the door without bothering to see if it was unlocked, shattering the glass and disappearing inside.

Christian raised his rifle and looked through the scope. Instead of the window where the shooter had fired from, he saw the retreating backs of men he'd shot during the riot in Paris. He blinked.

"They'll get him," Fluse said. "No need to waste your ammunition."

Christian nodded and lowered his rifle.

Emil was holding a hand over his wounded shoulder, but there wasn't much blood.

"No exit wound," said Fluse as he examined Emil's back. "We'll need to remove the slug."

"Wonderful," said Emil.

For the second time in a couple of minutes, the peal of shattering glass echoed in the narrow city street. This time, it was punctuated by a body hitting the ground.

The man wore civilian clothes and lay writhing on the cobblestones, reaching for a rifle that had landed near him. Christian ran over, kicked the rifle away, and covered the man with his own.

This man had attacked the Marauders. He'd shot Emil!

The trigger felt comfortable against Christian's finger. It was ready to gently squeeze and put an end to this. But all he could see was the man who'd been kicking Otto falling to the ground.

Christian lowered his rifle and blinked again.

"I know him," the sniper said as he tried to stand. "Know . . . him. One of us." He fell to one knee, then groaned as he fell onto his side. He was losing a lot of blood.

Miller ran out of the bakery, nearly knocking Christian over. "Is he—?" He stopped when he made eye contact with the sniper.

"You," the sniper said.

Miller raised his rifle, but Fluse stepped in and knocked it down. "What are you doing?" he asked.

"He tried to kill us!" Miller shouted.

"Use your head. Someone sent him. We need to learn who, and he's no threat now."

"Get that cart over here so we can carry him back to headquarters with Zimmerman," Christian said. "We'll interrogate him there. Move! There might be more snipers!"

Emil was already on a cart; it had room for a second person.

"Were they any others?" Fluse asked Miller.

"What?" Miller stuttered. "No. Just him."

"Are you sure? What happened up there? Did he jump?"

"Uh, yeah. He jumped."

The sniper shouted something unintelligible as Christian and the other Marauders heaved him onto the cart. Christian picked up the sniper's weapon and spotted a blood-soaked envelope. Miller lunged for it, nearly knocking heads with Christian.

"Oh, you have it?" Miller said. "I can carry it."

Christian stuffed the envelope into his uniform pocket. "I have it."

Fluse wrinkled his brow as he eyed Miller.

"So the sniper didn't make it?" Emil asked as he gingerly lowered himself into his chair.

"Bullet wound to the abdomen, head trauma from the fall," Christian said as he took a seat directly across from the desk.

"Verdammt," Emil said, flexing his wounded shoulder. "We could have learned a lot from him."

"Stop moving it, or I'll bring the doctor back here with his sewing kit," Fluse said as he sat next to Christian. "He said the bullet didn't hit anything important, which surprised me since it hadn't hit your head. But you need to keep your shoulder immobile."

Emil frowned.

"But more importantly, we did learn something from the sniper," Fluse said. "That's why I wanted to have breakfast here, where we can talk in private."

"Do we need Grundig?" Emil asked. "Or do you not trust him?"

"I trust him, but I'd rather wait before cluing him in," Fluse said, then nodded to Christian.

"We found a letter on the sniper," Christian said, pulling the blood-stained piece of paper out of his uniform pocket. "It appears to be from Ritter."

Emil shrugged. "So we have concrete evidence Ritter sent him? But that's hardly a surprise. Why all the secrecy?"

"There's more," Christian said. "A lot more. It's addressed to the cardinal."

Emil sat back in his chair, wincing in pain because he'd forgotten his shoulder wound. "A threat?" he finally asked.

"No," Christian said. "An update. In *German*."

The Marauders had the cardinal now. They had him dead to rights. He was a sympathizer, and he was working with Ritter.

"Huh," Emil responded. "Have you ever met the cardinal?"

Christian and Fluse shook their heads.

"Me neither. I don't know his real name." Emil rested his chin on his free hand. "Now it appears he speaks and reads German. Again, hardly a surprise. A man who has risen to the position of cardinal has probably served in a few different places. He might even *be* German."

"The letter says they'll meet again," Christian said. "In the same place, tomorrow."

Emil squinted. "That can't be right."

"What? That's fantastic news. Ritter's coming here. Maybe even alone, since he'll be keeping a low profile."

"Ritter sent someone to kill me while they were carrying a letter telling us how to capture *him*? He may be arrogant, but he's not stupid."

"You think it's a trap?" Christian asked. Emil did have a point. Christian hadn't wanted to see it that way, and he knew Fluse hadn't, either. But now that Emil had said it out loud, it started to make sense.

"It's brilliant, really. The guy kills me and gets away. I'm dead. He kills me, you catch or kill him, you find the letter and make fools of yourselves searching the cathedral and his residence. He fails, we capture him, and here we are, talking about searching the church tomorrow." Emil stopped to sip his coffee. "If there's one thing we can count on, it's Ritter believing he's smarter than us."

But Christian couldn't help but wonder whether Emil was wrong. What if Ritter had been overconfident? What if the sniper had been expected to deliver the letter before the shooting?

Christian groaned out loud and held up his hands in frustration.

"I get it, Christian," Emil said. "We don't want to miss a chance to stop Ritter. And if the cardinal is working with him, we need evidence. So we'll post someone to keep an eye on him, but they won't do anything other than take notes. There may be an advantage to knowing they're cooperating without tipping them off."

"And that brings us to the next problem," Fluse said.

"What?" Emil asked.

"We have to deal with the fact that we have an informant," Christian said. "The shooter knew the route we'd be taking. He picked the right place to be. This was planned."

Emil sighed.

"And I think we may have a candidate," Fluse said.

Wait. Fluse was going to discuss this *now*? Christian had thought he'd wanted to wait.

"Who?" Emil asked.

"My . . . Miller," Fluse said. "Stefan Miller."

"Miller? Gefreiter Shut Up? Really? Are you sure?" Emil slumped back, then winced in pain before looking up at Fluse. "You must be if you'd even bring it up."

Fluse crossed his arms and looked down at his feet. "First of all, only a few people were aware of the trip to the radio station in advance. You, me, Beckenbauer, Grundig, and Miller."

"Hmmm. That is interesting. Either our spy has a way to send word to Ritter very quickly, or . . ."

"And Miller's been acting erratic for a while now. I wrote it off to being far from home for so long, and the stress we've been through. But . . . I don't understand how or why the shooter went out the window, especially after he was already shot in the gut."

"What does acting erratic mean?" Emil asked. "I trust you, Fluse, especially when it comes to evaluating your troops. But we need to be very sure before we make any moves here."

Fluse nodded. "He was adamant about going with Beckenbauer on the reconnaissance up north. I finally had to pull rank to get him to stop. At the time, it seemed to be all about his desire to pay Ritter back and be involved."

"But now you wonder. Makes sense."

"And I thought he was going to strangle the gang member who tried to steal our cart a few weeks back, right after he heard me tell Beckenbauer to leave a man alive. I was willing to think it was him just reacting in the heat of the moment. But after yesterday . . ."

Emil nodded. "I get it."

"So that would mean he's working with the gangs . . . or with Ritter," Christian said.

"It doesn't need to be just one or the other, does it?" Fluse said.

Christian cocked his head.

"Ritter could be working with the gangs and the church *and* have an informant here. He wants chaos in the city. He wants to keep us off balance. Why not play everyone against each other?"

"That's a good point," Emil said. "But it doesn't have any bearing on whether Miller is the informant. I don't want to lose a valuable man, and I'm sure you don't, either."

"I appreciate what you're trying to say," Fluse said. "But I . . . we need to be clear-eyed here. It makes sense, at least until we have a better theory."

"Okay," Emil said. "Then here's what we're going to do."

CHAPTER 19

NOTRE-DAME CATHEDRAL, PARIS
FRANCE

f Ritter was going to meet with the cardinal, it would be either at the cathedral or back at his residence, after he went home from the service. So the next day, Emil's plan was to post Marauders at both locations.

The first problem was finding people to do that without tipping off Ritter's inside man. Christian and Fluse needed a way to effectively run a secret mission without tipping off the rest of the team. They'd needed at least two more people they could trust. Emil couldn't do much with a wounded shoulder, and pulling Grundig in would set off too many alarm bells.

Now, Fluse was watching the residence with Madame Curie, while Christian covered the cathedral with Jean, one of Madame Curie's close associates. The two of them would attend Mass and do their best to keep an eye out for anyone who didn't fit in. It was a tall order, but it was the best they could do without attracting too much attention.

Christian wore a hat and, much to his chagrin, was forced to shave off his mustache in the hopes that it would make him less recognizable. He had wanted to take the residence, but Fluse's French skills made him a better candidate for that.

Inside the cathedral, Christian sat on one side, and Jean took the other. The crowd was thin, probably because of the gang violence over the past few days. Christian politely acknowledged the greeter, dipped his hand in the holy water, made the sign of the cross, and found a seat that would be close enough for him to observe the communion line.

Mass had been a part of Christian's life for more than eight years, and the rituals were muscle memory—something he could take part in without thinking. But that didn't stop him from thinking about the memories that surfaced as he performed those rituals.

Emil and Fluse had been quick to dismiss Christian's antipathy toward the church, but neither of them had been raised in a Catholic orphanage. They didn't understand what that meant, and they wouldn't have believed him if he told them. They thought army training was difficult, but they had no idea what it had been like to grow up the orphaned child of Evangelisch parents in a Catholic home for children.

The time came for the Eucharist part of the Mass. Christian removed his hat and joined the line to go before the monseigneur and the cardinal. It had only been a few years earlier that he'd sworn to never kneel at an altar again. He should have fought harder to watch the residence instead of coming here.

Christian went with the first group, keeping his head down and resisting the urge to look out at the rest of the worshippers. Feeling dizzy, he knelt at the railing before realizing he'd been holding his breath.

He lifted his head to receive the Eucharist and heard the monseigneur gasp in recognition. Then came the wine, and Christian noticed the first major difference between Mass at Notre-Dame and back home in Germany. The wine here was cloyingly sweet, almost sickeningly so.

Finally, the cardinal came with the blessing. The child inside Christian considered surreptitiously crossing his fingers, just to prove that he wasn't a willing participant. But he forced himself to tolerate the man's hand and meaningless blessing. He told himself this cardinal wasn't one of the people who had called him a worthless, cursed, damned child.

Maybe the cardinal was different. Maybe he actually believed the message of peace and brotherly love that he preached. Maybe he could tell Christian that shooting nine men in a few minutes was okay.

Christian held his breath again, nearly stumbling when it was time to stand and file back to his seat.

Then, almost as soon as he sat down, Christian saw Miller.

The other Marauder was in the line for the Eucharist. He patiently waited with the rest of the worshippers in his group, eyes down like a faithful supplicant. Then he accepted his bread from the first priest as if he'd participated in the right a thousand times before, and sipped from the chalice the monseigneur held.

When had Miller gotten here? Was he even Catholic?

The cardinal faced Miller for the blessing. Miller briefly turned his gaze up to the church leader. Was there something behind that eye contact? A hidden message? An agreement to meet later?

Miller returned to his aisle on Jean's side of the nave. It would be difficult to follow him from where he was. Did Jean recognize him? Christian had only given him Ritter's description, not Miller's.

Mass proceeded slowly. It was agonizing for Christian. When it finally wrapped up, he watched as the cardinal exited via a door on one side of the altar. Miller couldn't follow him that way without attracting attention. He'd have to exit with the rest of the worshippers.

And then what? Did Miller have a way to meet the cardinal on the cathedral grounds?

Christian exited his aisle and worked his way through the crowd, hugging the wall so that Miller's view of him would be obscured if he looked his way.

Miller was patiently waiting in his line to leave the cathedral.

Christian kept one eye on him while following his group out. Then he picked up a telltale fragrance of aftershave, and the monseigneur appeared in front of him.

"A change of heart?" the holy man said with a warm smile.

Miller was getting away. But pushing past the monseigneur would only attract attention.

"Yes," Christian lied. "I wanted to attend and see how it felt. It was wonderful, but I need to . . ."

The monseigneur's brow wrinkled, and he crossed his arms. "Christian, can we talk for a minute? I know you need to get back to work, but this is important."

The monseigneur had a pained look in his eye. Whatever it was he needed, asking hadn't been easy. But Christian needed to know where Miller was going, and this was a waste of time.

Jean was waiting over by the door, eyeing Christian but smart enough to not approach and attract attention. The monseigneur might know who he worked for.

"It's about the villages," the holy man implored. "It's very important. I wouldn't bother you if it wasn't."

The villages? Well, Christian would still have something to bring back to Emil: Miller had been here instead of Ritter.

"Okay," Christian said.

The monseigneur looked around for a moment. "This way," he said, leading Christian to the confessional boxes and ushering him into one. He entered the other side and sat down.

So much for this being quick.

"I am not sure how to say this," the monseigneur started, then fell into silence.

What could this man possibly want to say to Christian? The last time they'd spoken in private, Christian had insulted him and sent him away fuming.

"I'm not even sure you are the right person to talk to, since you don't trust me," the monseigneur went on. "But since you're here on your own, Christian, maybe I can confide in you."

Christian hadn't been in a church for years, and now that

he'd finally returned, it was to take confession from a monseigneur? He might have been the killer, but the monseigneur needed *his* advice.

"I learned yesterday that there are supplies for the village," the monseigneur said. "Plenty of supplies."

"Really? So the cardinal has been . . ." No. If Christian phrased it that way, it might start an argument. "Lied to? There's been enough to feed the villages all along?"

"Yes. I thought you might understand." The monseigneur's face was barely visible behind the screen, but Christian could make out his wan smile. "I think someone has been lying to him. I was visiting a family near the warehouse district a few days ago. They lost someone—a very dear, very faithful, son—and I was there for counseling. I passed the warehouse where we used to pick up our supplies. It was open and *selling* tomatoes. Crates and crates of them. Our tomatoes! It's just so dreadful."

Christian sat back on the tiny wooden bench. This was evidence that the supply lines had never been interrupted, as the cardinal had claimed. But it wasn't proof that *he* was lying. It might have been the suppliers. But either way, there were supplies for the villages, and now the cardinal would look like a liar or a fool.

"Can the Marauders investigate this, Christian?" the monseigneur asked.

"Yes, yes," Christian said, tamping down his excitement. "Of course, Monseigneur. If we can find out what's happening, we can feed the villagers again. Have you discussed this with the cardinal?"

The monseigneur was silent for a long time. "No," he eventually said. It was clear that he didn't want to discuss the subject any further.

"Is there anything else you can tell me?" Christian asked. "Do you have an idea who might be behind this?"

"The shipments were managed by a wealthy member of the church. Here is his name." The monseigneur handed Christian a piece of paper before continuing. "Please be discreet. He is a highly respected member of the church, and I don't want to embarrass him."

Embarrass him? If this man was responsible for cutting off the villages, as the monseigneur seemed to suspect, his reputation would be the least of his worries.

"This is helpful, Monseigneur," Christian said. "I promise that we will speak to you before we do anything more than investigate."

"This is the place," Christian mumbled to himself as he reached the unmarked warehouse, a squat brick building where he'd picked up fruit, vegetables, and salted fish many times before.

It fascinated Christian to see how different the banks of the Seine looked and felt just a kilometer from the Marauders' headquarters. Here, the sickly sweet stench of rotting vegetables vied with fresh fish and manure. It was still early in the day, so carts were jostling for position while carters and vendors quibbled over weights and rates. Most of the carts were drawn by horses, but a few were pushed or pulled by men.

Fluse had stayed behind at the Marauders' headquarters to keep an eye on Miller. He and Christian had been ready to confront him over his appearance at the church, but Emil wanted to wait until they learned more about the spurious supply shortage. But Emil's shoulder was still too sore for him to ride, and bringing Jean to the warehouse might arouse suspicions, so Christian was visiting alone.

Absentmindedly, Christian scratched his stubbly upper lip as he opened the door. Another week or so, and his mustache would be back to normal.

A tall man clad in overalls and an apron was mopping the floor. Even though it was early, the place had been picked clean.

"Jacques?" Christian asked.

The man looked over from his mop and answered in French.

"Parlez-vous Allemand?" Christian asked.

"Oh! Maraudeurs! Wait a minute." Jacques dropped the mop in a nearby bucket and went into a door on one side of the warehouse. A moment later, he emerged with a man who wore a perfectly pressed business suit. This second man clearly hadn't done any warehouse work for years, if ever.

"Maraudeurs?" the second man said as he approached, his arms outstretched. "You are ready for supplies? I haven't heard from the cardinal lately. I'm sorry, we sold everything today, but I expect some excellent squash tomorrow."

"Mr. Gambon?" Christian said, recalling the name on the monseigneur's note.

"Gambon? Moi?" The man laughed. "No, I am Pierre, one of his assistants. Gambon is on holiday this month."

"I'm glad to hear you have supplies now," Christian said. "We just wanted to check before sending a cart."

"Now?" Pierre looked puzzled. "We've always had supplies. Has there been some sort of misunderstanding?"

"No, no," Christian said. "Of course not. We'll have a cart here tomorrow. And don't worry about the cardinal. We'll talk to him. Thank you!"

If nothing else, the Marauders could start feeding the villages again.

CHAPTER 20

THE MARAUDERS' HEADQUARTERS, PARIS, FRANCE

Emil took a long sip from his coffee cup, stopping to survey Christian and the other Marauders in his crowded office—Fluse, Grundig, and finally Miller—before finally speaking. "So, that concludes our normal business," he said, "leaving just the abnormal bits." He nodded to Fluse.

Christian edged toward the door, making sure he could block it if need be. This might not go well, but it needed to be done if they were going to get the confession Emil wanted.

Fluse had insisted on being the one to broach the topic of Miller's attendance at Mass. The Panzer commander was taking the situation very personally; and rather than disqualifying Miller because of a conflict of interest like Christian would have, he was giving the Leutnant free rein.

"Why were you at the cathedral yesterday, Stefan?" Fluse asked, his voice close to cracking.

"What?"

Fluse crossed his arms. Grundig quietly coughed.

"How is this anyone's business?" Miller protested. "I went to Mass. So what?"

"You're Evangelisch," Fluse said.

"Maybe I changed my mind," Miller said, wiping sweat from his brow.

"And maybe you didn't," Emil said. "You have to admit it's suspicious. Our relationship with the cardinal is . . . tense right now. You've got plenty of churches to choose from, including Evangelisch services right here at headquarters."

"Suspicious?" Miller asked. "You're having me followed, but I'm acting suspicious?"

"Nobody said you're being followed," Christian said. "We said you were seen at the cathedral."

"You stay out of this!" Miller said, taking a step toward Christian. He was a big man, but Christian was ready to take him on. Miller had betrayed them. He'd pushed the sniper who'd shot Emil out the window to cover his tracks. He'd wanted to join Christian on the trip north, probably to turn him over to Ritter. Christian could lay him out right here.

But that would short-circuit the interrogation.

Emil stood behind his desk, his arm still in a sling. But it was Fluse, with a hand on Miller's shoulder, who turned Miller away from Christian.

"And you!" Miller said to Fluse. "You're accusing me—"

"We're asking," Fluse said. "But your reaction isn't helping."

"Helping what?" Miller spat. "Feed more French people? Help your new best friend accumulate more power? You've forgotten everything, haven't you? You're a German officer! But you're over here, building some sort of international army with Zimmerman. *Zimmerman!*"

Fluse stepped back, his jaw open and his eyes wide with shock.

"At least Ritter remembers where we're from!" Miller finished.

Emil sat back down behind his desk and sighed. "So, you're relaying intel to Ritter through the cardinal?" Emil asked. "Or do you have another way to talk to Ritter and deliver messages to the church for him?"

"You think I'm going to tell you?"

Fluse leaned back on the desk, his hands shaking. "How could you?" he asked.

Miller shrugged. "How could I? How could *you*? You lined up under this traitor without so much as a thought."

The room fell silent.

"How do you talk to Ritter?" Grundig asked. "We'll figure it out eventually, so you may as well tell us."

"No, you won't figure it out," Miller said. "And I won't tell you."

But Christian knew they needed that information. They needed him to talk.

"You will if we make you," Christian said.

Miller laughed. "Zimmerman won't let you torture me, Beckenbauer. Don't embarrass yourself. When Ritter doesn't hear from me tonight, he'll . . ." Miller stopped and crossed his arms.

"He'll what?" Emil asked.

Miller said nothing.

"Now you finally shut up," Emil said ruefully. "If only you'd figured that out back in the trenches. How are those boots, by the way?"

Miller uttered a profanity.

"Well, now we know something is up tomorrow," Emil went on. "We already knew that the supply lines were never interrupted."

Miller dropped his arms to his sides and gawked at Emil.

"Oh yes, that didn't come up in the regular meeting, did it?" Emil said. "Someone was lying about that. We're not sure who Ritter got to, but he engineered it. Did he not tell you?"

"Of course he did!"

Fluse put the palm of one hand up to his face, then dropped it and stared at Miller. "You knew. He ran those villages out of food, and you went along with it?" Fluse's voice was so loud at the end that Emil gestured for him to lower the volume.

"Who cares about them? Who cares about feeding foreigners? We should be home, protecting the fatherland."

"Then why is Ritter over here, playing games with the cardinal?" Emil asked.

"Because once he takes Paris, he'll turn east with the Martians and take Germany," Miller sneered.

"With the Martians?" Fluse asked. "They're going to conquer Germany and just turn it over to him? Do you hear yourself, Stefan? You're talking about overthrowing your own country with the help of alien invaders. It's lunacy!"

Miller turned away from Fluse, and Christian realized this was a waste of time. Either Miller was insane, or he was blinded by hatred.

"We need to talk to the cardinal," Christian said. "Miller's got nothing to tell us."

"The cardinal won't tell you anything," Miller said without looking up.

"Because he's loyal to your cause?" Emil asked. "Or because he's in the dark? What did you do yesterday? Pass him a note? Meet him after Mass?"

Again, no response from Miller.

"Well, it's clear Ritter's going to attack Paris at some point," Fluse said. "And after that, he has his eyes on Germany. At least Miller told us that much."

Miller shifted on his feet, and the room fell silent again.

"So, we'll take the Panzers up to Ritter's headquarters," Grundig said. "They've never won a battle with those primitive automobiles. You said they had four Wanderers, Christian? I like those odds. We have four Panzers now, and I'll finish the fifth this week."

Miller stared at Grundig in disbelief.

"Oh yes," Grundig said with a black grin. "We have four already. I must have forgotten to tell you."

Miller stared at him balefully.

•   •   •

"Where is Miller?" Christian asked when he returned to Emil's office a half hour later, after searching Miller's room.

"The storeroom we used for your last prisoner," Emil said. "It's easier to keep him there. Now that you're done, I can have his bunk moved down there."

"So we'll do a court-martial?" Christian asked. As far as he was concerned, Miller had to serve as an example to anyone else who was thinking about turning traitor.

"We've got more important things to worry about," Emil said. "What did you find?"

"Yes, what did you find?" Fluse chimed in as he stepped into Emil's office. He had protested when it had come time to search Miller's room, so Christian had done it alone.

Miller might have been a traitor, but he was still a proud member of the German Army. His room had been spotless, ready for an inspection that would never happen with Emil in charge. Christian could have bounced a coin on his bunk. The floor gleamed, and Miller's spare boots glowed. The windows were clean to the point of being transparent. It was a little frightening, to be honest.

But one of Miller's desk drawers contained two things that might be hints: a pack of Gauloises, and a box of matches with the name of a local nightclub. Christian now held them out for Emil and Fluse to see. "This is all I found," he said.

"Petit Bain?" Fluse asked. "I've never been there. Maybe it's where he meets Ritter?"

"Worth a shot," Emil said. "He said it would be 'too late tomorrow,' so he may have been planning to meet him tonight."

"Or the plans are already made, and it really is too late," Christian said.

"That might be true, too," Emil said. "All we can do is plan for the worst. Grundig is already working as fast as he can on the Panzers. We need to tighten security on our perimeter and be ready to defend the city. But that doesn't mean we can't watch this club tonight."

"I'll go," Christian said.

"Yes, you'll go," Emil said. "Your new, clean-shaven look will help. So will I. And so will Gerhard here."

Fluse nodded.

"And that's it for the club," Emil added. "I want to keep this discreet, and I don't want to risk having one of our men scare Ritter off."

CHAPTER 21
PARIS, FRANCE

Petit Bain was a hole-in-the-wall on the far side of the warehouse district from the Marauders' headquarters. Too far away to easily walk, and too risky for a horse or cart ride for someone planning to overindulge in wine, women, or song.

It was an excellent spot for a traitor to plan a meeting.

Petit Bain sat in a small retail district, surrounded by a tattoo parlor, a barber shop, rooms for rent, and a small eatery that served West African food. Everything an itinerant warehouse or dock worker might need between shifts.

The bite of grilled spiced meat and stale beer met Christian's nose as he passed the restaurant on his way to the club. Farm-grown meat was in short supply of late, so he didn't want to guess what was being grilled, even as his mouth watered.

The club was dark despite the early hour. Christian headed toward the corner farthest from the door, figuring that was what Miller would do. The jacket, one that Fluse said Miller most often wore when out on the town, was loose on Christian's smaller shoulders. But it might fool Ritter long enough for him to take a seat and start talking.

"Look out!" slurred a mountain of a man as he bounced off Christian's left shoulder.

"Désolé," Christian said, hoping that his first few French lessons from Fluse would pay off.

"Allemand?" the drunk asked.

Verdammt. "Non," Christian said.

The drunk eyed Christian for a moment, then shook his head and stumbled off.

Inside the club, Christian rushed to the first available table in the corner and signaled the waitress for a beer. Fluse was already at the bar, dressed like a warehouse worker, complete with a watch cap and torn canvas pants. Emil was waiting outside; he'd stated earlier that "Ritter would spot me from hundreds of meters away, especially with the sling on my arm."

Once his beer arrived, Christian nursed it, struggling to only check his watch once every five minutes. He wished he hadn't been so quick to leave Ritter's compound when he and Otto had infiltrated it. He might have learned more about how Ritter communicated with the Martians and a little bit about their plans.

Would capturing Ritter mean preventing an attack on Paris? Or would the aliens press on? Why did they think they needed help from humans? What was their endgame? Christian figured that the Marauders would convince Ritter to talk once they had him locked in a room next to Miller's.

Assuming Ritter would be here tonight. For all Christian knew, they might have been wasting their time here, instead of preparing for Wanderers to cross the Seine at sunrise.

Almost as if he'd read Christian's mind, Ritter sat down across the table from him. "Not your normal spot, Stefan," Ritter said.

Christian raised his gaze from his beer and locked eyes with Ritter. The cavalry captain stood up, only for Fluse's hand to catch him by the shoulder.

"Let's do this the easy way, Hauptmann," Fluse said.

Ritter sighed and sat back down. Christian reached across the table and pulled a pistol out of the officer's coat.

After a few moments, Emil sat next to Christian, placing a pistol on the table. "I thought that was you by the door," Emil said to Ritter.

"Well, this is a misplaced . . . what would you Francophiles call it?" Ritter gave a wry smile then. "Ah, a misplaced rendezvous. But a waste of time, nonetheless."

"Talking to you usually is," Emil said. "But I'm interested in your friends, not you. You're coming with us."

"And if I don't?"

"Do you think it would break my heart to shoot you here?" Emil asked. "It would be regrettable, but only because you might have some useful information. But we have Miller, we know you've been communicating with the cardinal, and a kindergartner would even assume you'd move on Paris at some point. So do you want to live to see tomorrow, or not?"

Tying Ritter to the chair in the storeroom next to Miller's probably wasn't necessary. He was a large man, but too pragmatic to put up a fight when surrounded. Still, Christian had found it satisfying, and Emil hadn't argued when he'd had done it without being asked.

Ritter's wrists were now bleeding. The cavalry captain, clearly unaccustomed to being treated this way, was still pulling against his bonds after ten minutes. "You'll pay for this, Zimmerman," he said.

"I really doubt that," Emil said. "I may die in the next few days when your 'friends' arrive, but I don't think they'll spare a moment thinking about you. We're food, not friends."

"Not all of us. The ones smart enough to work with them will have a place in the future. You're just too wrapped up in yourself to realize it."

Emil laughed. "*I'm* too wrapped up in *my*self, says the man who believes he's so important the invaders will spare him," he said, still chuckling. "I shouldn't laugh, though. I'm the one who thinks it's worth the effort to try to talk to you."

Ritter growled and struggled against the ropes again. Emil was deliberately teasing him, Christian realized. Riling him up. Would that get him talking? Emil knew the man well, it seemed, but all he was doing was infuriating him.

"Miller's in the next room," Emil went on. "Well done, by the way. He's more loyal to you than me, even though he and I go back to the Somme. But as loyal as he is, he's not very bright. He already let slip that you have something planned for tomorrow. What is it?"

Ritter stopped struggling and smiled. "You'll never figure it out."

"So, it's not a Martian Attack?"

Ritter frowned. Maybe Emil's approach might work after all.

Emil picked up a chair with his good arm and sat it across from Ritter. He lowered himself into it slowly, balancing his coffee cup in his good hand. "Would you like a cup?" he asked as he held it up for Ritter. "It's going to be a long night."

"Only if you untie me," Ritter said. "I won't be fed like a child."

"I'm pretty sure Beckenbauer can take you on, and he'd love to. But I have two armed men outside, and I told them how little your life means to me." Emil cocked an eyebrow then. "Understood?"

Ritter nodded.

Emil tilted his head to Christian, who untied Ritter. The ropes came free easily, but Ritter still rubbed his wrists as Emil poured him a cup of coffee from a nearby steel pot.

"It's good stuff, but we don't have any milk," Emil said as he handed Ritter the cup. "Sugar?"

Ritter shook his head and sipped from the steaming cup.

"Excellent," Emil said. "Let's be civilized. How did you come to be allied with your 'friends'?"

Ritter raised an eyebrow.

Was Emil hoping that getting Ritter talking would lead to him revealing something? Christian agreed it was an interesting gambit. Emil probably didn't have the stomach for torture—and neither did Christian, if he was honest with himself.

"We're doomed, remember?" Emil added. "And we have all night. What harm will come of telling us what happened after Reims?"

Ritter sat back in the chair and looked up, as if thinking.

"I mean, we can grab some clubs and start a more traditional interrogation, if you want," Emil said.

"Fine," Ritter said. "Fine. I saw you use Grundig's Panzer to take out those Wanderers. And then he—" Ritter pointed to Christian "—shot Wegener, and I knew it was over. So I took my men and left Reims."

So Ritter had fled. But Christian knew that pointing it out would shut him up.

"We camped a few kilometers away, close enough to see the battle for the city," Ritter continued. "Grundig's new weapon won that battle for you."

"No argument there," Emil said. "It wasn't a battle on points. Thousands are still alive."

Ritter sniffed. "I was ready to head back to Germany when Wegener's contact, Chuchan, showed up at my door, so to speak."

"Chuchan? Wegener mentioned that name before he—"

"Before he died from this man's cowardly shot?" Ritter said, pointing to Christian again.

"Cowardly?" Christian said. "He was taking shots at us. What were we supposed to do?"

Emil held up a hand toward Christian, prompting him to stop. "Who is Chuchan?" Emil asked.

"Some foreigner who works for the aliens."

"We're in France," Christian said. "We're all foreigners here."

"You know what I mean," Ritter said. "An outlander. He's

from somewhere up north, in Russia. A native. They picked him up when they landed some ships there in 1908."

Emil and Christian made eye contact, then went back to Ritter, who continued, "He's the one who contacted Wegener after he took over in Reims. What I told you back in that village was true. They arranged those supplies for us, and they were . . . displeased with how Wegener was using them. You did them a favor." At that, Ritter grinned. "But you made up for it by protecting Reims. So they sent Chuchan to find me and make a deal. I help them with you and Paris, and I get part of Germany."

"I still don't understand why they need help from you or this Chuchan at all," Emil said.

"They don't tell us much. But I get the impression they learned from the first invasion. Microbes might have ended it, but it wasn't effortless before then, either. They struggled a bit."

"So, they're playing a long game."

Ritter smiled and nodded. Christian noticed how getting him to talk about strategy—and, more importantly, himself—took him off his guard. He grabbed the third chair in the room and got comfortable.

"So, this Chuchan," Emil said. "He's a native? Maybe from Siberia?"

"Yes!" Ritter said "That's it. That's what he said." He held out his cup for more coffee. Emil topped it off, then called for a guard to get more from the kitchen.

"And he spoke to you?" Emil asked. "A Siberian native who speaks German?"

"Not very well," Ritter said with a laugh. "Outlanders."

Emil grinned. "Yeah. Outlanders." The mirth didn't reach his eyes. "Of course, your allies are outlanders, too. Out*worlders*, one could say. How's their German?"

"They don't speak," Ritter said. "They use a machine. It puts words on a piece of glass."

"Words on a piece of glass?"

"You have to see it to understand."

Christian hoped that wouldn't be the case.

"So, if they don't say much, this was all your plan?" Emil asked. "Coercing the cardinal into cutting off supplies to the villages? Sending someone to assassinate me? Turning Miller into a spy?"

Christian noticed how Ritter met Emil's eyes when Emil mentioned the shooting attempt. "Yes," Ritter said.

"So, you did force the cardinal," Emil said. "Good to know."

Ritter frowned. "It wasn't hard, you know. He's no saint."

Christian, unable to help himself, smiled at the unintentional play on words.

"You don't understand, Zimmerman," Ritter said, holding out one hand. "The Martians are using men like me to speed things up, but they *will* succeed. It's inevitable. Go back with me. Talk to them. They'll work with you. They don't hold grudges."

Emil sat still, not answering Ritter. Heat rose in Christian's face as silence enveloped the room for what felt like minutes. Was Emil really considering it?

Eventually, Emil sighed once, then again. Ritter shifted in his chair.

"No!" Christian finally shouted when the pressure became too much. "Never! Emil, we won't work with them!"

Emil spun around to face Christian, his brow wrinkled in confusion and surprise. "Of course not. I just needed a moment to collect my thoughts."

He turned to face Ritter again. "Even if I did believe that their victory was inevitable, I would resist. I'd have to. It's my duty as . . . as a human. But I don't believe it, anyway. They're forced to use men like you here. They're playing similar games in the United States."

"It's a shame you didn't go back to Germany, Ritter," Emil said. "They could use you. You could be a fine soldier. I think you were once, better than I'll ever be. Maybe it was Wegener who ruined you."

"What do you mean 'they could use me'?" Ritter asked.

"They could. They said they needed more cavalry when we spoke last week." Emil shrugged then.

"You're spoken to home?"

"The provisional government. In Berlin. They may even send troops to us."

Ritter looked down at his feet.

CHAPTER 22

GOUSSAINVILLE, FRANCE

The Wanderer towered over the trees, frozen in place like an absentminded banker searching for glasses that were pushed up on his forehead. It broadcasted a short blast on its horn, then stood still for a few more seconds before proceeding north by northeast at an achingly slow pace.

Christian knew that whoever was in the Wanderer couldn't see him. Yet he still clutched his horse's reins, doing his best to keep the horse and himself concealed in the shade of the barn.

"Is it gone yet?" Louis asked. He was crouched near the ground halfway down the barn wall, too afraid to look for himself.

"Almost," said Lage, the only other Marauder on this mission with Christian. Lage was young—still a boy, really. He'd wandered into the Marauders' headquarters a month ago, his uniform tattered and torn, his sandy brown hair standing on end. The boy had walked alone from the Marne to Paris. His entire unit had been wiped out by the Martians.

Three days had passed since Ritter's promised event. Today, Emil had sent four men with a cart and a single Panzer to deliver food, and two men with a single cart to install the radioflashes. The rest were on guard at headquarters, while Emil and Fluse were heading to the cardinal's for a "social visit." Emil had cut Christian off before he'd had the chance to volunteer for that duty.

"No ravageurs with them," Christian said, still looking out from the barn.

"Huh?" Lage asked.

"Just thinking out loud. No ravageurs. We made it all the way here without seeing one of their cars. If they're looking for their leader, they're being very quiet about it."

The Wanderer stopped and hooted again. Another appeared from the north, nearly sprinting toward it. It reached the first in less than a minute, and they hooted between each other before the first Wanderer lifted a tentacle, the mirror for its heat ray gleaming in the midday sun.

"Is it getting ready to attack?" Christian asked.

Before anyone replied, the hum of a heat ray sounded, and a beam struck the second Wanderer on the underside of its barrel-shaped body. It stumbled, nearly losing its balance before recovering and returning fire, pointing its aiming mirror at the ground.

"What the hell is going on?" Lage asked.

Christian peered through his binoculars but only saw the two Wanderers. A heat ray fired from below them again, striking only the empty air, while they fired back. Soon, they were engulfed in smoke. Had they ignited some trees? Nearby buildings? What were they fighting? The supply team had been sent to the south that morning, so no Marauder Panzer should have been nearby. Was it a splinter from Ritter's group? Troops from Berlin?

Whoever it was, though, they were an ally of the Marauders.

"I'm going over to see what they're doing," Christian said. "Stay here."

He rode toward the conflagration, dismounting when the smoke and dust the Wanderers had kicked up were too thick to safely ride any further. When he finally reached the skirmish, his jaw dropped in disbelief.

An armored Mercedes was dueling with the Wanderers. Was this a family feud? The ravageurs and the Martians were fighting each other? Or had someone stolen the car?

Whoever was driving the car was good, skillfully dodging the Martian blasts while a man wielding the heat ray repeatedly hit both Wanderers. Smoke was rising from their fuselage, while the car remained unscathed.

The car passed near Christian, forcing him to dive behind a pile of burning scrub to avoid being seen. He reflexively grabbed his M98 and sighted the vehicle. He scanned the car as it slowly circled the Wanderers and found two, three, four gaps in the homemade armor.

The car was probably driven by an enemy, but it was fighting two more enemies. Enemies whom Christian's rifle was nigh useless against. Maybe it was better to let them fight.

The car darted through the legs of a Wanderer while its heat ray raked its underbelly. The alien walker split open and collapsed into a heap. Christian silently cheered. One down! But what would happen if the car took out the other Wanderer? Would it go for the village? Or flee to Paris?

Maybe its drivers were potential allies. Should Christian wait? He and Lage still had two radioflashes to bury. Their cart had a heat ray mounted on it. Christian could bring it within range and help with the battle.

But the Wanderers and the armored car had better mobility than a horse-drawn cart laden with two radioflashes and a power unit for a heat ray. Even if Christian managed to help take out the Wanderers, he didn't know if that car was driven by allies or enemies.

But . . . Christian could wire up a radioflash, drop it there, and ride far enough away to trigger it. It would take out both enemies, and then he'd learn why they were fighting, assuming the implosion left at least one of the men alive.

The men in the Mercedes were skilled warriors, Christian could tell. They alternated between charging the Wanderer and dodging its shots, picking away at its armor with carefully fired blasts from their weapon. But the surviving alien must have learned from its partner's demise, since it was preventing the car from getting close enough to cut it open with a sustained shot.

Christian ran back toward the cart. The fire had spread, forcing him to pick out a different path in the smothering smoke and dust. Guiding the cart this way would be difficult. But even if the battle ended while he was moving, he'd take out the victor and try to figure out why they were fighting.

And then the enemy might find the carnage and learn that the Marauders had these new, smaller, deadlier weapons.

That wasn't the plan, and Christian knew it. Emil would want him to observe the battle and report back. But if he did trigger the new weapon, it would eliminate another Wanderer, protect Goussainville, and help learn why those men were fighting the aliens.

Christian went back to his vantage point. The battle raged on. The smoke was clearing, but the car was moving slowly. One of its wheels had sustained damage from a hole or tree root.

A blast from the Wanderer caught a rear wheel on the Mercedes, paralyzing it. It traveled across the side of the car, stopping over the passenger compartment and staying there long enough to incinerate the occupants. Bile rose in Christian's throat as the car burst into shards of fractured steel.

Then the Wanderer limped away from Goussainville, smoke billowing from its water tank body.

"We would have destroyed all three of them with one of these," Lage said, pointing to a radioflash after Christian returned to the barn and explained what he'd witnessed.

"Yes, but then what?" Christian asked.

"What do you mean?"

"We'd be short a weapon, and they would know we have these things."

Lage looked confused.

Christian pulled a map of the area, unfolded it, and found Goussainville on it. He marked a spot where they were standing and labeled it with the number 4441834. "Let's get this thing wired up and buried," he said. "Then we need to explain to Louis how it works and give him this combination code."

CHAPTER 23

THE MARAUDERS' HEADQUARTERS, PARIS, FRANCE

"Why isn't the cardinal in a room next to Ritter?" Christian asked as he arrived at Emil's office the next day.

Emil shifted in his seat. "Because Ritter threatened him. Cutting off the villages wasn't his idea."

"Why didn't he come to us for help?" Christian asked, raising his hands in frustration

"Sit back down. This isn't a fight. He's guilty of being afraid. Ritter broke into his room and threatened him in his bed."

"That's an excuse, not an explanation. Assuming it's the truth, of course. We lost weeks because he shut things down and clammed up."

"So we lock him up in prison?" Fluse asked.

"The monseigneur wouldn't have hidden what was going on with us," Christian said. "And you can't deny the cardinal might jump at a deal that meant getting the Resistance out of the way."

"He might, but we can't prove it," Emil said before taking a long drink of coffee.

"Do we have to prove anything?" Grundig said.

Coffee dribbled down Emil's chin and onto his desk. "Excuse me?" he asked.

"Do we have to prove anything? Paris has no courts. We already have Miller and Ritter in custody, and there's been no court-martial or charges. Why would we need them for the cardinal? He's certainly guilty, even if he only complied out of fear."

Christian sat back down with a half smile. "Exactly," he said. "He's a risk. The monseigneur should be running the church, at least until they can reach the Vatican."

"Would the monseigneur go along with that?" Fluse said with a frown.

"We can ask him," Christian said, hoping to keep the idea in play.

"Ask him if he'd be okay with us locking up his boss so he can take charge?" Emil asked. "And if he went along with it, that would make him . . . more trustworthy?" He laughed coldly before stretching his arms over his head and massaging his healing shoulder.

"He was the one who came to me in the cathedral last week," Christian said. "It wouldn't be coming out of nowhere."

"I think it might be worth pursuing," Grundig said.

Emil frowned and looked down into his coffee, sighing deeply before responding. "Are you sure you're thinking this through? I don't have any loyalty toward the cardinal, but many in the city do. We're already dealing with riots all over the city. Unseating him might make things much worse."

Christian rested his elbows on his knees. Emil wasn't wrong. The monseigneur had quieted that riot a few weeks ago, but only with the authority of the church behind him, not his popularity. The Marauders taking the cardinal into custody might be seen as a coup, regardless of the reason.

But the cardinal had worked with Ritter. Christian knew he couldn't be trusted. It might only be a matter of time before Chuchan paid him a visit.

"What if we ignore him?" Fluse asked.

All eyes fell on him.

"We know where the supplies come from," Fluse went on. "We've already sent out two convoys. Just cut him out. We may be able to make deals with a few more suppliers. Leave the rioters to him, and we'll handle the villages." He shrugged then.

"That might work," Emil said.

It was a good idea, Christian agreed. The cardinal would stay in control, but with reduced power. He wouldn't be able to starve the villages any longer. "We'd still need to keep an eye on him," he said.

"Of course," Emil said. "I can talk to Madame Curie and ask if she can post some of her people at the cathedral and by his residence."

"Are we sure this still won't have consequences?" Grundig asked. "Will he like losing his influence on the shipments?"

"He was quick to give it up when Ritter told him to," Christian said.

"Has he contacted us about resuming them?" Fluse asked.

Emil shook his head.

"Well, I guess it's settled," Christian said.

"Good," Emil said. "We'll continue with the shipments and leave the cardinal alone for the moment. Now, Christian, tell us more about what you saw yesterday."

Christian recounted his story about the Wanderers and the armored Mercedes. Emil had heard it already, but it was news to Grundig and Fluse.

"A battle between Ritter's troops and the Martians?" Fluse said.

"We can't be sure," Christian said. "The car was incinerated. We have no idea who was operating it or why it was there."

"Wegener failed them," Grundig said. "And now Ritter has failed them. Maybe they're done with humans. Or at least humans from the German Army."

"There's not much we can do for now, other than finish getting the devices ready for an attack," Emil said.

"I'll be done in a day or two," Christian said. "Then I'd like to go see Ritter's camp again."

"That was my thought," Emil said. "I don't want to lose you if the Martians finally attack Paris, but it's either you or Gerhard who has to go there."

Christian was going to make sure it was him.

CHAPTER 24
PARIS, FRANCE

Christian decided to install an extra pair of radioflash units near Issy with Lage. This kept them out until later in the day, but would let him get underway to Ritter's camp a day earlier. He'd thought the late work would lead to lost sleep, not imminent combat. But as they'd entered Paris from the west, hoping to take the direct route through the city to the Marauders' headquarters, their shortcut had stranded them in the middle of another riot. Buildings on both sides of the avenue were now engulfed in flames, and the chatter of gunfire echoed from ahead.

Christian guided the cart down an alley and brought it to a halt. The closest river crossing wasn't far, only a few blocks north and east. But the main avenue had been taken over by skirmishes between gangs, and he was familiar with the neighborhood. Did it make more sense for him and Lage to take the long way around? Try to pick a way through corner buildings and alleys?

"Why don't we try to fight our way through?" Lage asked.

"We don't want to use the heat ray any more than we need to," Christian said. "It could make the fires worse than they already are. And while it's certainly more deadly than a gun, the gangs could still overpower us with sheer numbers."

This made Christian wonder what Emil would have done if he had been there. Once he thought it over, he added, "Let's try to find a safe spot to wait for things to calm down. Somewhere that won't burn down around us."

He led Lage and the horses down the alley and thought about going back in the direction they'd come from. Heading back out of the city seemed like a good option. The alley exited onto another avenue. They turned west again, and Christian hoped it might lead toward the river and a crossing to safety.

They made it a few meters, past a bucket brigade extinguishing a burning bakery, before shots flew over their heads. Christian raised his rifle to return fire before realizing it would only make him a more interesting target. Lage swung the heat ray around, and Christian waved him off, leading the cart into another alley instead.

"That was close," Lage said.

Christian opened his mouth to answer, but a voice further down the alley spoke first. "Marauders?"

Christian spun around, leveling his gun toward the voice.

"No shoot!" an elderly woman shouted as she held up her hands. "No shoot!" She was standing in front of a huge open door. "In here!"

When Christian and Lage entered through that door, Christian realized the building was an ancient stable, with walls of stone and a hardwood frame supporting slate shingles. He had lost touch with his faith in God many years ago, but this was enough to make him silently give thanks.

"We stay here until fighting stops," the elderly woman said in rough German. Her graying hair was up in a neat bun, and her apron was stained with flour. She was standing next to a man roughly her age, and two children: a boy and a girl, each about ten or eleven years old.

Christian jumped off the cart and gestured for Lage to help him pull the stable doors closed.

"Are we sure we won't end up trapped in here?" Lage asked.

"No," Christian said. "But we've been trapped in worse."

"It's those damn Maîtres Rouges," the old man said in fluent German with a familiar accent.

"Badische?" Christian asked.

"Willstätt. But I moved across the border after the first Martian Attack." The old man was standing close enough to Christian that he could make out a faint scar on one of the man's well-weathered cheeks.

"Then you fled here after the second Attack?" Christian asked.

"No. We moved here about a decade ago. Too old to keep a farm. Our son runs this stable. Taxis and cargo carts. He must be stuck on the other side of the trouble."

"And these rioters are Maîtres Rouges? Are you saying Serpent has men all the way over here?" Lage asked. "I thought he controlled the northern and western parts of the city."

"He controls nearly two-thirds of Paris," the old man said. "And he's probably hoping to have the sixth arrondissement by tomorrow morning."

How did that happen without the Marauders being aware of it? Had Christian and the others been so distracted by Ritter and the cardinal that they had missed Serpent's activities? He must have been rolling up the smaller gangs into his. He'd have a standing army by now.

"We need to stop him," Lage said, facing Christian.

Lage was right. If Serpent established a beachhead all the way over here, he'd control too much of the city. Had he taken the twelfth arrondissement already? Was Charlotte safe?

But what could Christian and Lage do just then?

"We have a single cart, armed with a weapon that will do nothing more than make the fires in this neighborhood worse," Christian said.

The old man nodded.

"I can run," Lage said. "I can find my way across the river to headquarters and try to bring back some Panzers. Or you can go. You're second-in-command, and Zimmerman listens to you."

"You don't want to split up," the old man said before pointing at the heat ray on the back of the cart. "Can you disable this weapon?"

Grundig had recently added what he called a "fusible link" to the units. It was fashioned from a large piece of soft, conductive metal. When the fusible link was taken out, the circuit that activated the ray would be broken. A thief would need to not only realize which piece was missing, but also know how to replace it.

"Yes," Christian said. "Why? You want us to leave it? You know of a way out of here?"

"The catacombs," the old man replied. "They'll take you north and west. If we're lucky, the riots haven't spread there, and you can walk to your headquarters from there and pick up the cart when the excitement is over."

"The catacombs?" Lage asked.

"Tunnels. Tombs. They're hundreds of years old. Most of the gang members are from out of town, and they either don't know about the catacombs or are too afraid to go down there." At that, the old man grinned.

Shots hit one of the heavy stable doors, startling everyone. The children ran into the old woman's arms.

Christian popped the link out of the heat ray and put it in his pocket.

"Follow me," said the old man, and led everyone to a side door. Christian sent Lage to the back of the group while he stayed up front with the old man.

"We'll take Jardin du Luxembourg," the old man said. "It's dark, so we can cross without any risk of being seen. Then we'll just need to make it to the stairs."

They crossed the avenue and went through a gate that opened

onto a walking path through public gardens. The old man had been right; the gardens were dark, and the natural cover from the trees made Christian wonder if they should just stay there.

But as they crossed the gardens, they walked right into trouble. Three men wearing Maîtres Rouges colors were headed in the other direction.

"What's this?" one of them said, eyeing Christian's uniform. "Maraudeurs? And sympathizers?" He grabbed the old man by his arm.

"Let him go," Christian said as he raised his rifle.

"You won't do anything," the Maître said. "Not in front of the children."

Images from Christian's last encounter with rioters flashed before his eyes. The Maître was right; he didn't want to kill more civilians, especially not in front of children.

But the old man was the children's grandfather, wasn't he?

"I don't want to," Christian said. "But I will." He would have to thank Fluse later for the latest French lessons.

The Maître sneered and smacked the old man, knocking him to the ground. The old woman screamed and clutched the children as she covered their eyes.

Christian put a bullet through the Maître's heart.

The old man climbed back onto his feet and stared at the dead gang member as the other two Maîtres ran away.

"I'm sorry you had to see that," Christian said, glad that the night hid the single tear running down his cheek.

"Nothing new to me," the old man said. "I saw worse at the siege of Metz." He touched his wife, who was crying, on the shoulder and spoke to her. "We need to go. Now."

Christian and the rest of the group ran to a gate that took them out of the gardens. From there, they crossed the avenue and entered a doorway.

"This way," the old man told Christian.

The group descended a long set of stairs for minutes that felt like hours to Christian. They exited into a clearing where a group of villagers were already huddled around a single torch.

"Most people have refused to come down here since the first Attack," the old man explained as he picked up another torch, lit it, and handed it to Christian.

"Why is that?" Christian asked.

"The Martians pumped their Black Smoke down here. You can still see the powder in a few corners."

No wonder no one from the Resistance had mentioned the catacombs to Christian and the other Marauders. They wouldn't want to rely on these tunnels during an alien attack.

"This way," the old man said then, leading their group down the tunnel at a quick pace. "It's less than a kilometer to the northern exit." They had already descended at least 200 steps, based on Christian's guess, but the carefully formed walls could have been in any aboveground stone structure. The tunnels felt safe.

The first tunnel ended, and when the old man led the group to the right, Christian gasped as his torch illuminated the far wall. It was covered, floor to ceiling, with human skulls. *Will you shoot us, too, Christian?* they seemed to say. *Too bad we're already dead.*

"Oh yes, the gallery," the old man said with a snicker. "The catacombs aren't for transportation. They're burial grounds. If only the people knew what was under their feet."

Christian shivered but pressed on. The group eventually walked down an arched hallway and reached another intersection.

"Your exit is over there," the old man said, pointing in the direction Christian and Lage needed to take. "The tunnel takes a gradual climb, and you'll find a shorter flight of stairs to the street. Look out for the abandoned prison, though. The gangs use it for a headquarters. If you need a drink before you go, there's a good well to the right."

"Let's get a drink first, Lage," Christian said. "It's been a long day."

"So when are they coming?" the old man asked as Christian and Lage scooped up water in their hands.

"Who?" Christian said, his brow wrinkling.

"The Martians. They'll run out of villagers at some point."

"Heinrich!" his wife scolded. "The children!"

He shrugged. "They need to know what they're facing."

"I . . . I'm not sure," Christian said. "It might be soon. You have somewhere to go?"

Heinrich laughed. "There's nowhere to go, son. All you can do is make it hard for them."

Christian finished his drink, then thanked Heinrich for his help and headed for the entrance with Lage.

"Is he right?" Lage asked. "We're all going to die?"

"He didn't say that," Christian said.

"Didn't he?"

Lage wasn't wrong. But instead of worrying about himself, Christian realized he was more worried about Charlotte and Patty.

CHAPTER 25

THE TWELFTH ARRONDISSEMENT, PARIS, FRANCE

The Blue Bandannas, as Christian referred to them, were on the same corner they had been a few days ago. But this time, the men standing in front of the group wielded clubs and hammers, while another hung back with a double-barreled shotgun and a gleeful sneer.

The tallest gang member met Christian in the middle of the street and challenged him in French. Christian didn't comprehend a single word.

"I'm here to check on a friend," he said, using the line he'd practiced with Fluse. He had about three hours to check in on Charlotte and Patty before he needed to be back at headquarters for a planning session. The riot and the old man's words in the catacombs had left him wanting—needing—to be sure they were okay.

The first Blue Bandanna spoke again, slowly enough that Christian understood this time: "You don't belong here. Go home."

All Christian could think of doing was repeating, "I'm here to visit a friend. To make sure she's okay."

Shotgun stepped forward then and waved his weapon back and forth. "Go away," he said in German. "Go away."

"You understand German?" Christian asked. "I'm just here to check on a friend." He held up his hands to show that he wasn't a threat.

"Go away," Shotgun said before drawing back the hammers on his weapon.

Coming alone had been a mistake for Christian. Coming without a translator had been an even bigger mistake. But coming with nothing more than a revolver? That might have been a fatal error.

"Please," Christian said. "I just want to be sure she's okay—"

"You're here to see Charlotte?" a tiny voice said.

Christian spun around, careful to keep his hands up. An elderly woman holding a wooden crate overflowing with vegetables was standing behind him.

"Yes!" Christian said. "I'm here to make sure she's okay."

"I saw you with that other man a few days ago. What happened to the other one? The one who used to visit?"

"He's . . . gone."

"I see. Well, I believe you when you say you're here to check on her. I'll get you in." The elderly woman spoke to the Blue Bandannas in French then. They broke out into a debate, but finally the men parted to let her and Christian through.

"Let me carry that," Christian said, and hefted the crate onto his shoulder.

"They're good boys," the elderly woman said. "They're just trying to protect us."

"I understand. My friend usually does the translation for us, but he couldn't come today."

The truth was, Fluse couldn't come. Emil had banned all nonessential travel into the city, and Fluse had hung back to cover for Christian.

"I don't know how much longer you Marauders plan on staying, but you should think about learning the language," the woman said.

"Your German is very good," Christian said. He could tell she wasn't a native speaker, but her grammar was perfect.

"I'm a schoolteacher. This is your lucky day."

"Yes, it certainly is," Christian said with a chuckle. "Thank you."

"Of course. I live in the same building as Charlotte. I'll knock on her door and let her know that you are outside waiting."

Christian and the elderly woman approached number forty-two then. She eyed him to see if he'd object to being left outside.

"That would be perfect, thank you," Christian said.

Charlotte appeared at the door a moment later. She nervously looked right and left as she let him in.

"Christian," she said as she led him down the hallway. "I didn't expect to see you."

"I wanted to be sure you're safe," he said as he followed her to her door and then into the kitchen.

"I . . . we . . . are . . ." Charlotte was holding the coffeepot when she choked back a sob. She handed Christian the coffee cup and gestured for him to take a seat.

"What's wrong?" he asked.

An older man wearing dusty coveralls entered the kitchen. He was graying at his temples and hadn't shaved in a few days. "The Maîtres Rouges have been visiting us," he said. "I'm Francois, Charlotte's father." He held out a hand for Christian to shake. "Please forgive my rough German. School was a long time ago."

Christian took Francois's hand and nodded. "Christian," he said.

"The Maîtres are 'recruiting,' or at least that's what they call it," Francois said. "They've been here and at my job on the docks a few times already. They want an oath of loyalty, and they are making men do jobs to prove it."

By then, Charlotte had sat down across from Christian with a mug of coffee, dabbing her eyes with a handkerchief.

"Jobs?" Christian asked.

"Robberies," Francois said. "Assaults and batteries."

"Wonderful. How are they getting past the men wearing blue? I only got here because your neighbor helped me."

"Those fools? They're putting on a show. It will get them killed. They can't guard every path into this neighborhood, and they're outnumbered at least twenty to one." Francois held up his hands then. "At some point, Serpent will decide it's time to send a message, and they'll be dead."

Gathering more intelligence on the Maîtres Rouges and the twelfth arrondissement was one of the excuses Christian had prepared in case he was confronted for leaving headquarters. He'd have to share this adventure at the planning session and risk the consequences. Serpent's group was everywhere and had to be stopped.

"They want *you* to join?" Christian asked.

"Yes," Francois said. "I know. I'm old."

Christian held up his hands to apologize.

"No, I understand," Francois went on. "But this isn't about how useful I might be. It's about fear. And they need bodies for the vanguard when they attack armed gangs like the Marauders. Why not a bunch of old men?"

Charlotte was quietly weeping, with her head in her hands. Patty walked into the room then and held up her hands for her mother to pick her up.

Serpent and his gang had to go, Christian realized. The meeting this afternoon would hopefully start that process. But Charlotte and her family, and countless more innocent city dwellers, were in danger.

"Are you going to work today?" Christian asked. "I can go with you—"

A thunderous pounding rattled the apartment's entry door.

"It's the Maîtres Rouges," Charlotte said. "I don't what they'll do if they find you here!"

Christian's heart raced. His throat felt dry, despite having finished his coffee. "They're here?" he asked. "Now? How did they get inside?"

The pounding rose again, followed by shouts.

"You need to hide," Francois said. "In here!"

He grabbed Christian's arm and pulled him into a bedroom that connected to the kitchen, then pointed at a closet. "Keep quiet, no matter what you hear. They'll kill us all if they find you!"

Christian squeezed into the closet, trying to make as little as noise as possible. It was small, but nearly empty. Any Maîtres that bothered to check the room would spot Christian as soon as he opened its door. Still, he kept the door cracked so he could hear the intruders.

The shouts grew louder, followed by the stomping of heavy boots. Either Charlotte was leading the Maîtres Rouges to the kitchen, or they had forced their way in. Cups and saucers rattled, presumably as the gang members helped themselves to coffee and food.

Various French voices alternated with Francois and Charlotte for what seemed like hours but was probably only a few minutes. They rose at one point, punctuated by a slap and the sound of someone falling to the floor. Charlotte shouted while a man grunted; it must have been Francois who had suffered the blow.

Christian's C78 pistol held six rounds. How many gang members were out there? Could he kill them all before they got him? Or Charlotte and Patty?

Patty. Did Christian want her to see him kill a bunch of men? What would that teach her?

The gang members left as abruptly as they had come, making Christian's choice moot. It was a few more minutes before Charlotte and Francois returned to the closet for Christian.

"What happened?" Christian asked Francois, who held a wet rag against his lip. "Did they hit you?"

"Nothing I'm not used to," Francois said. "But I will be joining them on a warehouse raid tonight."

Christian gaped. "You can't."

"What choice do I have? They'll hurt Charlotte or Patricia next." Francois sounded resigned as he spoke.

No. Christian couldn't let that happen. The Maîtres Rouges had taken Otto. Now they'd take Charlotte's father.

Christian sat down at the kitchen table again. What could he do? Put guards here? The Marauders didn't have the numbers for that.

Patty sat on her grandfather's lap, sobbing. For a moment, Christian could almost feel her rage and the heat of her tears as they ran down her cheeks. "Kill them," she said. "I want to kill them."

Patty still must have been recovering from losing her home and her father. If Christian let the Maîtres Rouges take away her grandfather, she'd never recover from it. There was only one choice.

"Come with me," Christian said. "You'll live with the Marauders until we figure out how to stop this gang."

CHAPTER 26

GOUSSAINVILLE, FRANCE

Goussainville was quickly becoming Christian's favorite village. He was on a first-name basis with nearly everyone, and it was one of the three or four villages that would celebrate whenever an electric Panzer rumbled into town.

It was a Sunday, and the children's choir was waiting for the Marauders in the market square. Church hymns were far from Christian's favorite form of music, but the celebration brought a smile to his face and helped him forget about the troubles in Paris.

Within a few minutes, the two supply carts were distributing food, and the Panzer was posted nearby.

"It's always nice to see you, Herr Beckenbauer," Louis said.

"Please, Louis," Christian said, shaking the villager's hand. "Call me Christian. I haven't been here since that battle between the Wanderers and the ravageur car. Have they been back?"

"No. Whatever they were fighting over, they've either settled or taken it elsewhere."

Louis led Christian over to a table and offered him a glass of apple cider. Christian took it with a smile. The cider was glorious. It was somehow tart and sweet at the same time. Each sip brought back memories of climbing trees, fields ready to harvest, and early football matches.

A little girl ran up to Christian and spoke in rapid-fire French, gesturing as if she was turning a wheel. Christian didn't understand a word she said, but he gradually realized she was the one who had nearly fallen into the well a few weeks earlier.

"She's explaining that she helped her father press this cider, Christian," Louis explained. "It's the first of the season."

The girl's jubilance was infectious, and Christian couldn't help but smile and laugh. She seemed to be about the same age as Patty, but still unburdened by the war and the Martian invasion that had interrupted it.

Emil hadn't been pleased when Christian had returned to a locked-down headquarters with a family of three in tow. Even so, not taking them in had never been an option, especially after Christian had explained how he knew them and why he'd brought them in.

Emil had also been extremely concerned to learn Serpent was active in yet another arrondissement and recruiting civilians for raids. The Marauders were, in effect, being dragged into defending Paris from a second enemy: one from within.

Still, the villages needed the Marauders' support, too, especially with fall nearby. The harvests were starting, and winter was on the horizon.

The Panzer sprang into life suddenly, charging toward the opposite end of the village from where they had entered.

"Take cover!" Christian told Louis and the girl, and ran off after the Panzer.

The vehicle was already at the edge of the village, firing its heat ray when another bolt of heat flew past it and into the village square.

Martians? Or ravageurs?

Christian ran to one side of the road for a clear view. Two armored cars were firing on the Panzer while driving in a serpentine pattern, making it difficult for the Panzer to track them. It was one of the German Panzers, not as fast or maneuverable as the Renault that Christian had used when he'd faced the armored automobile not too long ago.

Eventually, the Panzer connected with one of the cars, which burst into flames as it careened off the road and into a field. The other auto blew past the Panzer and into the village.

The Marauders needed a prisoner, and it was doubtful there'd be any survivors in the car that was already down. Christian held up a hand to the Panzer, hoping the Marauders inside would understand and let him disable the active auto before it did any serious damage.

Then, as if reading his thoughts, the armored car opened fire on the church. The people inside must have thought they'd have plenty of time before the Panzer could turn around, so they spun the car around and made ready to fire on the Marauders' vehicle.

Bile rose in Christian's throat. He chambered a round in his M98, then trained his sights on the car. He could make out the opening where the gunner and the driver looked out. Then he changed his mind.

He squeezed off three shots. The mirror shattered in a million pieces just as the Panzer turned and trained its ray on the armored car.

"Get out of the car, or we'll cook you in place!" Christian shouted.

The car reversed at speed and attempted a three-point turn. The Panzer fired.

Verdammt! Christian had purposely been bluffing. The Marauders needed a prisoner, not more dead.

But the Panzer was firing at one of the armored car's wheels, melting it into slag. The car flopped onto one side.

Christian wished he was inside the Panzer so he could praise Fluse on a job well done.

The armored car's doors opened. The two men climbed out, their hands in the air.

"Are there any more of you?" Christian said with his rifle on his shoulder.

"No!" the one who'd exited from the driver's side said.

"Why should I believe you?"

"It was just the four of us. You killed the other two in their car. We escaped a few days ago."

Christian lowered his rifle in shock. "Escaped?"

"I don't believe them," Grundig said.

"I'm not sure I do either," Emil growled. Fluse shook his head in agreement.

The men had quickly gathered in Emil's office as soon as Christian and Fluse had returned with their prisoners.

"I did see that battle between one of the armored cars and a Wanderer a few weeks back," Christian said. "It's not hard to believe that Ritter's gang fell apart now that he's been missing for a few days."

"But mutiny?" Emil asked. "Ritter's a military man. He would have appointed a competent deputy."

"And he picked the wrong guy," Fluse said with a shrug. "Ritter may be a military man, but he didn't have the luxury of being choosy about who he recruited. Did you ask him what he thinks happened?"

"Why would he help us?" Emil said. "I wouldn't believe him if he did anyway."

"Well, sometimes a lie can expose a little truth," Christian said.

"Hmmm," Emil responded. "I'll think about it. But regardless of what we may learn from talking to these foul-ups, it's clear that we need to visit Ritter's camp again."

"Is it a good time?" Christian asked. "With Serpent's men circling us?"

"Is that strategy I'm hearing?" Emil asked with a smile. "From Beckenbauer?"

Christian sat back in his seat, stung by the comment.

"Please!" Emil said. "You know I'm kidding! You're right, and I'm glad to hear it. 'Chase two rabbits and catch none,' my grandfather used to say. But we don't have any choice. We're fighting two wars. We have a decent idea of what Serpent can bring: many men, but armed mostly with sticks and some small weapons."

Emil stood up and started to pace. "But we have no idea what the ravageurs and the Martians are doing out there and what they have left. I'm not sure what we can do even if we do know, but I'd rather see the axe coming. Wouldn't you?" Emil eyed the other three men as he posed that question.

Christian nodded. So did Fluse and Grundig.

"Christian, you know the way to Ritter's camp, so you're going," Emil said.

Christian knew that would be tough, but it was possible.

"And I'll go with him," Emil added.

Fluse and Christian gasped, while Grundig burst into one of his coughing fits.

"That's ridiculous," Fluse said. "Serpent or the aliens could attack us at any minute."

"Yes, and you're the best man to run our defense," Emil said. "We need a man who can defend this compound without burning down or leveling the city. That's you, not me. My shoulder is healed enough for a long ride. And Grundig is in no shape for two or more days of hard riding. He needs to help you figure out what weapons we need and how to use them. I want two of *us* assessing the ravageur camp and making plans in person."

"Emil, we've talked about this in the past," Fluse argued. "You need to delegate—"

"I *am* delegating, Gerhard. I'm delegating the defense of this compound to you and Grundig. I leave tomorrow morning."

CHAPTER 27

SOMEWHERE NORTHWEST OF PARIS, FRANCE

"They're everywhere," Emil said.

He wasn't wrong, Christian knew. They'd seen at least a dozen Wanderers since leaving Goussainville, and they still had five hours of riding left. It would take closer to seven or eight if they had to keep rerouting or stopping to avoid the Martians.

Would it be like this all the way?

"I wish we could send word back to Paris somehow," Christian said. "But there's not much left between here and the ravageur compound. No one to send as a messenger."

"I'm not sure what the message would be," Emil said. "They're active, but they seem to be just milling around. Reminds me of the activity around Reims."

"That ended with an attack on the city," Christian reminded him.

Emil's only response was to set his jaw.

The latest Wanderer they'd sighted receded to the south and east, and they continued riding at speed for a couple of hours. The sun was high in the sky when they came across a group of people clustered around a disabled cart. They were a family: a man in his fifties, a woman, a teenage boy, and a younger girl.

The cart was resting on its side, with a bent rim on one of its front wheels.

Christian and Emil stopped their horses nearby, dismounted, and approached the family.

The man spoke at them angrily in French, standing in front of the cart with his arms spread open. He looked haggard, with a few days of salt-and-pepper beard on his cheeks, torn pants, and a half-tucked shirt. The woman and the girl cowered behind the cart, while the boy was trying too hard to appear menacing with a broken shovel.

"We're not here to rob you," Christian said in halting French, his hands held up in supplication. "Can we help?"

"You are soldiers," the man said in German that was nearly as rough as Christian's French. "Soldiers rob us already. We have nothing more."

Christian's eyes met Emil's. When Ritter had been in control, there had been a rhyme and reason to the ravageur raids. Robbing carts on the side of the road had never been part of his plan.

"No, we're not here to rob you," Christian said, holding up empty hands.

Emil placed his weapon on the ground in front of him, with the barrel facing away from the family, before holding up his hands. Christian unstrapped his rifle from his shoulder and did the same.

The man relaxed, but only slightly.

"Can we help you with that wheel?" Emil asked, and took a few steps closer.

The woman spoke from behind the cart. After a few moments, the man stepped aside and pointed to the cart. The woman dashed from behind it and hid behind the man.

"This isn't that bad," Emil said, looking at the wheel more closely. "If we take this off, we can probably straighten the rim with some leverage."

Christian carried pliers, oil, and brushes to augment the standard-issue cleaning rod for his rifle in his saddlebag. Though they were a little small for the job, he used the pliers to pull the pin that secured the wheel on the axle. But how would they straighten the rim?

Emil rummaged through a nearby stand of trees and returned with a few sturdy branches. He arranged them in different configurations, stroking his chin and muttering to himself.

Soon, the teenage boy could not control his curiosity any longer. He set his rusty shovel down and moved in for a closer look. Even the woman and the daughter seemed to relax as Emil and Christian jockeyed the wheel around the improvised jig.

"I thank you," the man said as Emil and Christian stopped for sips of water from their canteens.

Christian nodded.

"Where do you go?" the man asked.

Christian pointed northwest. "Scouting. Searching."

"Not safe. Big fighting. Martians fight men."

Emil shrugged. "We need to see."

"Martians are very dangerous, even for soldiers who rob us," the man said, shaking his head.

Christian couldn't argue that the Martians were the biggest threat, the source of all the death and destruction of the past few months. It was easy to forget that without the Martians, Ritter would have been a low-level officer in the kaiser's army, and Serpent would be in jail or selling stolen vegetables. But even though Christian was worried about what might be happening in Paris while he and Emil were away, it felt good to be on a mission that was at least partially concerned with the alien invaders.

After another half hour, the wheel was back on the cart and straight enough to get the family to Goussainville. Christian put the pin back in place to the sound of cheers in both languages. He and Emil then helped the family load their remaining belongings into the cart. Emil gave them directions and a hand-drawn map to Goussainville.

"You come with us," the man said. "Stay away from Martians."

"I'm sorry, I wish we could go with you. Goussainville is a special place. But we have to take care of something," Christian said. "We'll see you again."

The sun was low in the sky when Christian and Emil reached the hill that overlooked Ritter's compound. It was a gradual slope, but they took it slowly. The men and the horses were all tired by then.

Christian was daydreaming about opening a can of beans when the sharp bite of burning wood and Benzin brought him out of his reverie.

"Do you smell that?" Emil asked.

Christian nodded.

They crested the hill. Even though it was still light enough to see the valley where Ritter had built it, Christian couldn't believe his eyes.

The compound was a smoldering mess.

"Mein Gott," said Emil.

The trees that had ringed two-thirds of the area were burnt stumps. Black spots dotted the grounds, some large enough to be tents and others so small that they could only have been bodies. The line of armored cars was a row of twisted metal.

The Martians had turned on their hosts. The ravageurs might have been traitors to their nations and their species, but no one deserved this. Not even them.

Christian's palms were sweating so much that he nearly dropped his rifle when he hoisted it to view the carnage through the scope.

A few piles of debris were still burning. The attack had been recent.

Something in his scope's line of sight moved then.

"Survivor?" Christian said.

"Two," Emil said, holding field glasses up to his eyes.

"We need to go capture them."

Emil scanned the horizon. "There are no Wanderers in sight. So yeah, I guess we go." He sighed before adding, "Let's save some traitors, share our food, and try to resist the urge to beat answers out of them."

Christian urged his horse onward.

"Hold on," Emil said, pointing toward the ruins of Ritter's camp. "See those taller tree stumps?"

Christian nodded.

"One of our two ravageurs thinks he's concealed over there. He has what I think is an M98 with a scope."

"So do I," Christian said, hefting his weapon.

"The other one is lying near a burning car. He's wounded. We might not be able to get him out of there. So if we want a prisoner, we need to capture our erstwhile sniper intact, or at least intact enough to question him. Any ideas?"

Christian peered through his scope and found the shooter. He was sitting behind a tree stump, with only his lower body covered. He was young—only a boy, really. He picked up his rifle and scanned the area with his scope without checking the hill, then put it down.

"He has no idea how to cover a perimeter," Christian said. "And that's not his rifle. Someone else added that scope and either gave it up or is already dead. But depending on how resourceful he is, he may have a lot more ammo than I do. I need to outshoot him."

Christian scanned the area around the soldier. Next to him was a single crate of field rations and a water barrel. "He was smart enough to collect supplies or hide next to them," Christian said. "I have an idea. We need to get a little closer."

He and Emil rode back down the hill, stopping by a row of

trees at the bottom. Once there, Christian found a clear line of sight to the soldier and his supplies.

"I hope you know what you're doing," Emil said. "Those supplies might be tasty."

"Quiet," Christian said, then quickly put three rounds in a tight pattern into the water barrel.

The soldier turned toward where the shots had come from, shouldered his rifle, and fired back wildly. He stopped when his rifle was empty. His entire upper body was exposed. One shot from Christian, and this would be over. But Christian and Emil needed to learn what had happened here, and Christian didn't feel like killing anyone.

The soldier reached down for his pack, placed it on the stump, fished out a clip, and fed it into his weapon. He stopped for a moment when he realized he was kneeling in a puddle of water. He finished loading and started firing in Christian and Emil's direction.

"Whoa!" Emil said. "If we give him another hour, he might hit something."

Christian fired again, hitting the crate of rations. The soldier turned and grinned. He must have thought Christian was missing.

"Think he'll catch on?" Christian asked.

"Not at this rate," Emil said with the field glasses up to his eyes again. "Think you can knock his helmet off?"

"I'm not a circus performer. But you did give me an idea."

Christian's rifle still had two rounds left, so he fed in three more, then manually put a sixth in the chamber. He shouldered the rifle and sighted the pack sitting on the stump. "Time me," he said, waiting a second before firing. It fell from the back of the stump on the fifth round.

"Nine seconds," Emil said. "You're getting slow."

"You do better!" Christian said, still watching the ravageur through his scope. The youth's eyes were as wide as pie plates as he gawked at the pack on the ground, then back at Christian. He tossed the rifle over the stump, raised his hands, and stood.

"I guess he got the message," Emil said.

Christian found the second survivor underneath a dingy tarp, one of the few intact pieces of cloth in the perimeter. It was immediately clear that he could neither walk nor mount a horse due to the burns on his legs.

It was a miracle that the poor soul was still alive.

Christian was helping the man drink when Emil arrived with the sniper.

"Willi!" the sniper said. "Willi! You're still alive?" He ran to his comrade's side and knelt next to him. "I didn't know . . . I would have . . ." He burst into tears.

Christian handed Willi the canteen and stood up. Emil turned away.

The two ravageurs spoke quietly while Emil and Christian stood back at a respectful distance.

"He can't make it back with us," Christian said.

"I figured," Emil said.

"What do we do?"

"We can't leave him here. At some point, he'll be attacked by wolves or carrion eaters."

"What are you saying?" Christian asked.

"Put him out of his misery," Emil said.

"We can't!"

Emil raised an eyebrow. "Is it against your religion?"

Was it? Was Christian reacting to what had been imprinted on him as a child? Or the past few weeks?

"We have to help him!" the sniper said as he stood up and approached Emil and Christian.

"You were trying to kill us a few minutes ago," Emil said. "Now you're making demands?"

The sniper took a step back. "You're going to let him suffer? Or use him to interrogate me? What do you need to know?"

"No, we're not doing either," Emil said. "But maybe you should consider where you are, how you got here, and what you were doing just a few minutes ago."

The sniper looked at the ground like a scolded child. "Okay."

"Your friend can't travel, and we're not medics," Christian said, helplessly wondering if the boy had a better idea than Emil.

Emil walked over to Willi and knelt beside him. "Can you speak?" he asked.

"Yes," Willi said, gasping. "Help me."

"We're trying to figure out how."

"Give me a pistol."

"No, Willi," the sniper said. "We'll get you to a hospital—"

"Even if I could survive the trip, I don't want to. Please. Help me."

Emil walked over to his horse and pulled out of his saddlebag the M1879 pistol Christian had taken from Ritter. He checked the barrel and set the hammer. "You two may want to look away," he told Christian and the sniper.

"No!" the sniper said.

"It's not your decision," Emil said. "It's his."

Emil might have been right, but Christian knew that didn't make it right. They were helping a man kill himself. Christian opened his mouth to object but couldn't find the words.

The sniper dropped to his knees, bawling like a child.

Emil handed the M1879 to Willi, then calmly turned and walked away.

The shot reverberated across the open area, probably all the way to Paris.

The sniper was still weeping quietly as he stood and faced Emil and Christian. He wiped his nose on his sleeve. "This is Hauptmann Ritter's fault," he said. "He lied. He told us that Martians would work with us. He said they wouldn't kill us; they'd put us in charge."

"It's the Martians' fault," Christian said. "They killed your men."

"And he made it easier. He brought us to them!" The sniper looked even more like a petulant child as he shouted through his tears.

It was the fault of all the soldiers, Christian knew. The men had believed Ritter. They'd trusted a preening peacock. Believed him when he'd said that they were special and that the invading predators would treat them differently from all the other prey. But that wasn't what the boy wanted to hear.

"Ritter is one man, and he's a prisoner now," Emil said. "The Martians killed your friends, and they're getting ready to attack Paris."

The sniper tilted his head. "A prisoner?"

"Yes. Our prisoner, back in Paris. Now, show me where we can find some entrenching tools. We need to dig some graves before we get some sleep."

The moon was high in the sky before Christian, Emil, and the sniper made camp on top of the hill. The boy was still sobbing in his borrowed bedroll when the sun rose the next morning.

CHAPTER 28

THE MARAUDERS' HEADQUARTERS, PARIS, FRANCE

No one would ever accuse the Marauders of mistreating their prisoners. To Christian, Ritter looked like he was in better shape than he'd been the day they'd brought him in from Petit Bain. He was perched in an office chair, his clothes perfectly pressed, his mustache neatly trimmed, his hair combed over with military precision. And he wasn't just sitting in the chair. He was presiding in it. Christian felt like Ritter was holding court, like he was one of his subjects.

Maybe that was because Christian—along with Emil, Fluse, and Grundig—was sitting across from Ritter, his back to the door as they all waited for him to speak. Christian and Emil had returned the night before and they were still bleary-eyed from the ride home, but they had no time to waste. They needed to talk to Ritter right away.

"I don't believe you," Ritter finally said.

Emil laughed. "You don't believe us? You think we made this up? Your men are dead, Ritter. Dead. Your 'friends' slaughtered them. You led your men into the hands of the Martians, and except for a handful who got wise, they're lying in your compound northwest of here in a pile of ash."

"You're a liar, Zimmerman. You and your tribunal here."

"A tribunal would be three people, Ritter. Not four. Stick to military theory," Fluse quipped.

"Whatever. You're lying. You can go now."

"Oh? We're dismissed?" Emil asked. "Why? Are you expecting your tailor to show up for a fitting? How long do you think you can keep freeloading off us? I'm tempted to let you go and see how long it takes you to come back begging for your room. But first, I want you to meet someone."

He turned and knocked on the door. It opened, and two other Marauders escorted Brandauer, the young sniper Christian and Emil had brought back from the north, into the room.

Brandauer saw Ritter and exploded in a paroxysm of rage. Emil and Christian had to stand to hold him back. After a minute, Emil gave up and nearly carried the boy out.

"What a terribly disturbed young man," Ritter said. "Should I know him?"

Christian's mouth dropped open. Was Ritter serious? Did he not recognize one of his men? Or was that a callous bluff? The stereotypical German officer was aloof and deliberately stayed separate from his men, but the ravageurs had lived together in that camp for weeks.

"I almost believe you, Ritter," Emil said. "You *are* a bad enough officer to not recognize one of your men on sight."

"I think we should leave Herr Brandauer in here with Ritter for a few minutes with the door locked and let them get acquainted," Grundig said.

Christian jumped at the sound of Grundig's voice. He was usually silent during their meetings, only offering opinions about technology or weapons. But there was history between him and Ritter, and Christian sensed it wasn't pleasant.

"I'm sure you'd like that, Grundig," Ritter said.

"At least admit that the boy would beat you to death before you raised a fattened fist, you old fossil," Grundig said with a wheezy chuckle.

"Like you would have a better chance."

"I would. I didn't lead that boy's best friend, Willi, to his death."

Ritter's face fell.

"So you know Willi?" Emil asked. "We buried him two nights ago."

Ritter looked away.

The door opened. A soldier stepped in, leaned in to speak into Emil's ear, and then stepped out.

"Fluse and I need to go take care of something," Emil said. "Christian, you and Grundig can keep Ritter company while we're gone. Maybe he'll have a change of heart."

Emil and Fluse left, closing the door behind them.

Ritter didn't move.

"Get Herr Brandauer," Grundig said. "I promise I won't let him kill Ritter."

He was smiling, but Christian saw no humor in it. Letting Brandauer in there unrestrained would be tantamount to torture, if not a summary execution. Ritter deserved it, but Brandauer might do it too fast for him to suffer enough.

They needed Ritter to talk, though. He knew how to talk to the Martians, and how to reach that Chuchan character.

"You ought to know that Willi was burnt so badly he asked for a pistol, Ritter," Christian said. "We gave him yours. He put it in his mouth and pulled the trigger himself."

Ritter's eyes flicked over to Christian, then away again.

"And Miller's next door. He heard about what happened out at your camp and tried to drink a bottle of bleach."

Ritter looked down, but his mouth stayed closed.

"How do you talk to the Martians, Ritter? They use some kind of machine? What do they say to you? What was the plan before you got yourself captured?"

Still nothing from Ritter.

Christian went to the door and opened it. "Bring Brandauer back in," he said.

Ritter faced the door, maintaining a mediocre poker face.

Grundig smiled as the two guards escorted Brandauer back into the room.

"Leave him with me," Christian said.

"Sir, he's—" one of the guards began.

"His arms are tied behind his back, and he'll cooperate as long as I'm here. Right, Klaus?"

Brandauer nodded.

The guards shrugged and left the room.

Christian kept one hand on Brandauer and closed the door with the other. "His arms may be tied behind his back, but I have a knife," he said as he pulled an ivory-gripped lock blade out of his pocket. It wasn't his grandfather's knife. That blade had been taken away from him years ago. "So what was the plan, Ritter? I'm going to count to five."

"You wouldn't," Ritter said.

"Zimmerman isn't here," Christian said. "One."

"Do it," Brandauer said. "He won't tell you anything. He doesn't know anything. He left, and his Martian masters wiped us out."

Ritter stuck his chin out in defiance.

"Two," Christian said.

Brandauer moved forward, forcing Christian to hold him with both arms.

"Let me go!" Brandauer screamed. "They're dead because of this coward!"

The knife clattered to the floor as Brandauer strained against Christian's grip. Ritter pushed his chair back a few centimeters but maintained a stoic expression.

Christian wanted to let Brandauer go. The boy would kill Ritter with his teeth if he had to.

Christian reached down for the knife, letting Brandauer slip forward a bit, but keeping a grip on him. Brandauer howled in frustration—

And Christian caught himself. He was falling into the same trap as Brandauer. The one he was afraid Patty would fall into.

He took a firm grasp on Brandauer and forced him to the door.

Ritter frowned at the floor.

"Take him," Christian told the guards as Brandauer cried out in frustration. Christian knew he owed him an apology and an explanation later.

"You win for now, Ritter," Christian said, turning back to him before he walked out the door. "Sleep well tonight. Try not to dream about Willi with your pistol in his mouth. Try not to think about the mess we had to clean up before we buried him."

"Word is the cardinal's still hanging in front of the cathedral," Emil said. "But no one from the Resistance can get near the place. It's surrounded by demonstrators and rioters."

Christian's mind reeled as he dropped into one of the chairs lined up in front of Emil's desk. Serpent had publicly executed the cardinal. It was hard to feel any pity for the man, but it was still a shock. Even in this post-Martian Attack world, a public execution seemed brutal. And attacking the cardinal was a bold move. The church had been one of the most powerful forces in France for generations.

"I don't believe it," Grundig said. "There's no way he did that."

"You sound like Ritter," Fluse said.

"Never say that again," Grundig snapped.

"Well, believe it," Emil said. "Serpent stormed the church and hanged the cardinal. Declared him a traitor to his species for collaborating with the Martians."

"Was he?" Grundig asked.

"Was who doing what?" Emil asked.

"Was the cardinal working with the Martians?"

"Does it matter?" Fluse asked.

Grundig shrugged. "It would be good to know."

"He was working with Ritter," Christian said. "They might have reached out to him after we captured Ritter."

"Well, if Serpent killed the cardinal because he was for working with the Martians, will he be looking for Ritter next?" Grundig asked.

"So now he has two reasons to attack us," Emil said. "There's no reason to think it's only a matter of time."

And since Christian had brought Charlotte and her family here to protect them, they were now in even more danger than if they'd stayed home.

CHAPTER 29

THE MARAUDERS' HEADQUARTERS, PARIS, FRANCE

The workroom on the third floor that Christian had selected for Charlotte and her family was unrecognizable. She had scrounged up complete bedroom and dining room sets, erected screens to give the workshop individual rooms, and even set up a cooking area on a workbench next to a window for ventilation.

Christian knocked twice, then cautiously let himself in to find Charlotte serving stew to her father and Patty. It was late in the day, and in the dim, waning light, it almost felt like visiting an apartment.

"Christian, have you eaten?" Charlotte asked. "I have plenty of stew here."

Christian had made a habit of visiting them every day, but this visit wasn't for dinner. He was there to explain how they needed to uproot themselves for the second time in two weeks. To tell her that by convincing them to relocate here, he'd exposed her family to an even greater danger.

But as Charlotte held out a bowl of rabbit stew spiced with black pepper to him, Christian knew it would be rude to refuse her hospitality.

"Um, sure," he said, sitting down at the table as Charlotte handed him the bowl.

"What's the latest word on the Martians?" Francois asked. "Do we know when they're going to come back here?"

Francois had gone to work for the Marauders the day after he, Charlotte, and Patty had arrived at headquarters. He was now tending the small vegetable garden in the morning and cleaning and maintaining weapons in the armory after lunch.

"Well, that's why I'm here," Christian said. "We're more concerned about the Maîtres Rouges right now."

"Really?" Charlotte asked as she finally sat down with her own bowl of stew. "Why?"

It hadn't been as easy for Charlotte to fit in. While a handful of women worked in the compound during the day, she was the only one who lived on the premises. On their third day after her arrival, she'd shown up at the armory unannounced. The armorer, too stunned to question her, had bragged about Charlotte's skill with taking down and cleaning an M98 by the end of the week.

"I guess by now you've heard what Serpent did to the cardinal?" Christian asked.

Charlotte nodded gravely.

"What did he do?" Patty asked her mother in French.

Patty was picking up German quickly, which made sense for a girl her age. But it made conversations like this difficult.

"He was very mean to the cardinal, and it's made everyone very angry with him," Charlotte said, making eye contact with Christian as she spoke.

"We were discussing why he . . . was mean to the cardinal," Christian said.

"I see. Please wait a moment, Christian." Charlotte turned to Patty then. "Do you want any more stew?" she asked in German.

Patty shook her head.

"Then go to your room and work on your reading."

"But I want to talk to Christian, too!"

"You can read to him after he finishes his dinner."

Christian smiled and nodded. Patty pouted but left the table, placing her bowl and spoon in the dish tub on her way out.

"Serpent said the cardinal was working with Martians," Christian said once Patty was gone.

"Do you believe him?" Francois asked.

Christian refilled his glass with water. Charlotte's stew was spicy. "Personally, I do. But that's not the point. Serpent hates the aliens, and he's killing anyone he thinks is a collaborator. The cardinal probably gave Ritter up. So as soon as Serpent figures out where Ritter is . . ."

"But attacking the Marauders would be suicide," Charlotte hissed. "Let him come!"

"It would be suicide for a street gang with a few dozen members to attack us. But it's a different story when we're talking about the man who's consolidated most of the gangs in Paris and can start a riot with the snap of his fingers."

Charlotte frowned.

"He can rally hundreds, maybe thousands, of civilians," Francois said. "Tell them you're harboring a traitor. He might even accuse you of collaborating with Ritter. How would the Marauders defend against that? Kill them all?"

Christian closed his eyes and tried to banish the mental image of dead bodies surrounding Otto.

"You want us to leave," Charlotte said.

When Christian opened his eyes again, he looked into those beautiful blue eyes of Charlotte's. "The Resistance can get you out of here," Christian explained. "Out of Paris completely. It's not safe here anymore."

"It's not safe anywhere," Charlotte replied. "I'd rather stay here."

"I don't want to leave, either," Francois said.

How could Christian make them understand? They'd seen plenty of destruction and lost family to the Martians. They'd been bullied by Serpent's men. But they'd never been in the middle of a firefight or withstood the chaos that had gripped the city for the past few weeks.

He held up his hands in resignation. "Outside of Paris, you only have to worry about the aliens. Here, you have the gangs *and* the Martians. You said that to me when we met. I should have helped you leave Paris instead of bringing you here. I'm sorry."

Charlotte smiled. "We have a home here. More of a home than that apartment. You don't have to be sorry. We're thankful, Christian."

The Marauders' headquarters might have been her family's home now, but Christian knew it could turn into a death trap if Serpent triggered a mob and used it to storm the compound.

"I think you'll find more of a home back outside of the city," Christian said. "The Resistance can take you to Goussainville. It's a lovely village. I've been there many times and made some friends there."

"If we wanted to leave Paris, we could go back to our farm," Francois said.

Their family's farm had been near Ritter's compound, where Christian and Emil had seen all those Wanderers. They wouldn't be safe there.

"I can't go back there," said Charlotte. "I already told you."

That settled that, at least for the moment.

"I hope someday we can all go home," Christian said. "But for now, you need to compromise."

"So you'll go back to Germany someday?" Charlotte asked.

Would Christian go back? He didn't have any family in Germany. He didn't have a home to go back to. Or did he? He only shrugged.

"But you like this Goussainville?" Charlotte asked. "You would live there?"

Christian sat back in his chair. He'd daydreamed about it a few times, but he'd never taken it seriously. What had Grundig said? The future was cloudy with all that had happened since the Martians had returned. Or since Christian had been drafted and sent to the front in Belgium, really.

But he would. He'd love to live in Goussainville.

"Yes," he finally said.

"So if we go, will you come find us?" Charlotte asked. "When you're finished?"

She was asking Christian to come with her. Did she really mean it? That was something he hadn't dared to dream of.

"You would want that?" Christian asked.

"You've helped us," Charlotte said. "And I've seen how you are with Patty."

"But do you really think this ever will be over?"

"I didn't say when it's over. I said when you're finished. That's up to you, not the Martians."

"I don't understand," Christian said. Was it the language barrier? Or did Charlotte mean that he should give up?

"You decide when you are done, Christian," Charlotte said. "No one said this has to be the rest of your life."

"I can't abandon the Marauders. We've protected one another since Reims. Many of us have been together since the start of the war."

"But you have to decide if you want to live for something more than fighting."

She was right, of course. Running from one skirmish to the next was easy. Finding something to live for was hard.

Patty walked back into the room. She was carrying her toy soldiers and the improvised Wanderer. "Can I play in here now?" she asked.

"Yes, you can," Charlotte said.

Patty sat on the floor and arranged her toys for a new war. "Let's get the Martians!" she whispered to herself.

"I promise," Christian murmured to himself. "I'll meet you in Goussainville."

CHAPTER 30

THE MARAUDERS' HEADQUARTERS,
PARIS, FRANCE

Serpent must not have thought he needed the element of surprise. He had announced that he'd be at the front gate to demand from the Marauders that they release "the German traitor" to him at ten in the morning.

The sun was still rising when a crowd started forming around the factory perimeter. But rather than being an invading force, they were a mass of eager onlookers waiting for lions to pounce on hapless Christians.

By 09:00, Christian was posted on the third floor of the main factory building, in what had been Charlotte's apartment. He was armed with field glasses, an M98 with a scope, and several boxes of ammunition. He scanned the crowd outside, but the closest thing he could make out to hostile intent was a few placards with French profanities aimed at German soldiers.

Charlotte, Francois, and Patty had been gone for three days. Enough time for them to get to Goussainville and send word back that they were settled in. Hopefully, Patty was already playing with the other children instead of toy soldiers and home-made Wanderers.

A flash of movement east of the factory caught Christian's

attention. He checked it with the field glasses. Men were moving in formation. Two columns of at least twenty, led by the unmistakably broad form of Serpent. They reached the edge of the milling crowd and forced their way through. In a few moments, the Marauders' defense plan would be put to the test.

Christian checked his gas mask. It was ready to go.

Grundig, as usual, had come up with the weapon they needed: nonlethal tear gas. Christian hated chemical weapons, but he had to admit that, in this case, gas was the most humane option. Serpent's best defense—a mob of innocent civilians—was already gathered around the Marauders. Shooting anyone who breached the perimeter would mean killing people who were there to watch the show or, like Francois, had been pressed into service.

The heat rays were all but worthless in Paris, since they risked burning the city down. They might be an option when the Martians were to attack, but in a riot they would add fire to the fuel. A relatively low-powered version of tear gas made for a decent compromise. The Marauders would wear masks, and the Maîtres Rouges would suffer.

Christian was posted on one side of the factory with orders to only shoot Maîtres who presented a clear threat. Would that mean shooting civilians? Would Christian know if he did? Did a red bandanna mean an aggressor or a decoy? What exactly was a clear threat?

Trench warfare was so much simpler.

Emil, the next best shot in the group, was on the other end of the building, minding the back entrance. Christian wondered if he was having an easier time dealing with his own orders.

The Panzers were posted in front of the gates, acting as roadblocks. Determined attackers could climb over them, of course, but they'd face the gas and Marauders with bayonets fixed to their rifles.

Serpent and his gang members reached the front gate at

roughly 09:30. It was a huge group, larger than Christian had thought when they'd pushed through the crowd. Maybe a few more men had joined in? They all wore the red bandannas, though. Very considerate of them to make it easier for Christian to know who to shoot.

One of Serpent's men had been carrying a crate. He placed it on the ground, and Serpent stood on it and raised his arms over his head. "Attention!" he bellowed in French. "Attention!"

His men chimed in, and after a few moments, the crowd grew quiet.

"We are here for the traitor and collaborator Ritter," Serpent shouted. "He is guilty of working with the aliens and misrepresenting his intent with the Maîtres Rouges. For these crimes, he will face the ultimate penalty—the same one already given to his friend, the cardinal."

The crowd cheered.

Whether the Marauders should bother trying to parlay, or even responding to Serpent, had been a matter of debate last night when word of the gang leader's announcement had reached headquarters. Christian had thought it would be a waste of time. Serpent was going to attack. Debate would merely delay the inevitable and risked pulling critical men, like Emil and Fluse, out of position and into greater danger.

Fluse had argued that debating with Serpent might knock the man off his guard. Grundig had wanted to hang Ritter on a pole in front of the gate. Emil had laughed at Grundig's suggestion before growing quiet long enough that he seemed to consider it, but he'd eventually agreed that any talk would be pointless.

Now, Christian placed his sights on Serpent, then on each gang member one at a time. He could make the shots. He could probably empty his rifle into them before the last target realized what was happening. But that would trigger a riot that the Marauders—and perhaps even the entire city—would never recover from.

Serpent looked at his watch. He made his announcement

again. His face was red, and he spoke sharply to his men. He didn't like being ignored.

Finally, after a few more minutes, Serpent raised his arms and shouted. The attack had begun.

Serpent fell back and out of sight. He was smart enough to realize the Marauders had snipers. His men literally jumped onto the gate. Christian watched them through his scope and was still trying to decide whether it was safe to take a shot when the first cloud of gas blocked his view.

It spread quickly. Screams rose from the crowd as they realized what it was and scattered in every direction. Was it a stampede? The men by the Panzer, following Grundig's carefully laid out plans, opened two more canisters to either side of the vehicle, obscuring the view even as the gas dissipated.

Christian's heart climbed into his throat as he saw one, then two, then three more Maîtres Rouges emerge from the cloud to stand on top of the Panzer. Their bandannas were wet and covering their noses and mouths.

One. Christian hit the closest Maître in the leg. The man dropped to the ground.

Two. Struck the next one in the shoulder.

Three more shots, and three more Maîtres were down. None were intended to be killing shots.

Christian had just finished reloading when he noticed a cluster of attackers crossing the courtyard and engaging the Marauders. Several of those Maîtres Rouges were armed, and the riot turned into a firefight.

One. Christian delivered a shot to a Maître's head. At least this one had been firing a rifle.

Two. Knocked the rifle out of the next Maître's hands. Not what Christian had intended, but it did look impressive. But there was no time for him to admire his work.

Three more shots. One miss. The smoke was getting too thick.

Christian wasn't lacking targets and was reloading for the second time when Emil shouted in frustration.

"What is it?" Christian yelled back. "Are you hit?"

"They've breached the back gate!" Emil said.

The Marauders had prepared for this possibility, but they'd hoped that Serpent hadn't. With their lower numbers and their hands tied by not wanting to kill civilians, the Marauders were already at a huge disadvantage. Defending the compound on two fronts was too much. They'd need help back there.

But Christian already had a job. He made five more shots. Four more Maîtres Rouges were down.

Time to reload again.

But the courtyard was nearly empty. Were the Maîtres Rouges gone? Based on the noise level, the battle had moved into the building.

Christian ran to the back window. Emil was already standing there, clearly thinking the same thing.

"You check on Ritter," Emil said. "I'll head to the lab."

This, too, had been part of the plan. Christian strapped his rifle across his back, pulled his pistol from his coat, checked it, and hit the stairs at a run, He covered two floors in a few seconds, then ran down the hall toward what had become the jail.

He turned a corner and nearly plowed into two Maîtres, dropping them with the pistol before they could fully react.

When Christian turned the last corner, he found both guards on the floor and Ritter's door open. The bite of the tear gas had made it to this area, but Christian didn't need a mask. Not yet.

The only thing visible through the doorway to Ritter's room was Serpent's massive back. The gang leader was shouting profanities and had both his giant hands around Ritter's throat. Ritter squirmed and tried to rake Serpent's face with his fingers, but Serpent shook him like a child's doll.

Christian emptied his pistol into Serpent's back. The gang leader dropped Ritter and turned in shock. He shouted louder this time, took two steps toward Christian, and dropped on top of Ritter like a puppet with its strings clipped.

Ritter gasped for air, finally drawing enough to scream, "Get him off me!"

Christian grabbed Serpent under the arms, but all he managed to do was cover himself in blood. Serpent weighed more than an overfed cow. He switched to the gang leader's feet; and after nearly a minute of struggling, shouting, and cursing, Ritter was free.

Ritter staggered to his feet, still gasping for air. Then he reached out with both hands and pushed Christian to the ground.

"I'll shoot!" Christian said, scooting to the door to block Ritter's way.

"That pistol is empty," Ritter said.

It had been Ritter who had taken Christian and the others to Wegener's camp, drafting them into a madman's army. It had been Ritter who had stood laughing in Hermonville after the same madman had used a heat ray to burn down a Gasthaus full of people. And, it had been Ritter who'd gone on to ally himself with the Martians after his leader had been killed.

Everything that had happened today—every man Christian had wounded or killed, every terrified civilian who was hit with tear gas—was because of Ritter.

And he wanted to run away?

"You're right," Christian said. "It's empty." Then he flipped the pistol so he could hold it by the barrel and struck Ritter across his nose with it.

Ritter collapsed to his knees, howling in pain.

Christian shoved a few rounds into the revolver and pulled back the hammer. "*Now* it's loaded."

Ritter raised his hands, still moaning.

"I'm not sure how many people I've killed today, but it was too many," Christian added. "And it was all because of you. But as much as I'd love to add you to the list, you're too useful."

Ritter sneered.

Christian held up the pistol to Ritter's forehead. "But resist me again, and you'll stop being useful. You're going to walk in front of me, and I'm going to tell you which way to go."

"And what if I'm shot?" Ritter asked.

The man always thought he had an angle, didn't he?

"Then you'll be buying me time," Christian said. "Now get moving. Turn left out the door." He positioned himself behind Ritter and pushed the back of his head with the pistol barrel.

They stepped out of the room, and Ritter had to step over one of the guards. Christian picked up a whiff of gas again and had an idea. "Take his mask and put it on."

"But I won't be able to see," Ritter whined.

"That's one good reason. The other is, there's tear gas outside, and I don't want to carry your fat ass."

Christian nudged Ritter with the pistol barrel again; and Ritter pulled the gas mask over his head.

"I can barely breathe with my nose broken," Ritter gasped.

"Well you can pull the mask off, and I can try to hit it again," Christian quipped.

They turned two corners before Ritter screamed, "Black Smoke!" He spun around, knocking Christian into the wall, and ran the other way.

Christian looked in the other direction. Ritter hadn't been lying. The hallway was filling with that deadly ebony cloud.

Christian took off after his prisoner.

Ritter must have found his way out of the building quickly, because when Christian barreled out of the door and into the courtyard, the other man was already there, about five meters clear of the door, leaning forward with his hands on his knees.

"Stop . . . there," Christian panted, holding his pistol out in front of him. But Ritter wasn't going anywhere, of course.

Christian was still fighting for air and resisting the urge to pull off his mask when more men wearing red bandannas around their faces ran out the door. They sprinted right by him, climbed over the Panzer, and fled the compound.

The courtyard was eerily quiet then. The ground was scattered with bodies, most of them wearing red bandannas. German Black Smoke was pouring out of the windows of the far side of the building, but a stiff wind was carrying it away from the courtyard.

Christian pulled off his mask and grabbed Ritter's. "Take off your belt and put your hands behind your back," he said, holding the gun to Ritter's face.

"I'm not going anywhere," Ritter said.

"I know. Now do it."

Ritter complied, and Christian wrapped the belt around his hands and secured the buckle.

"What if I lose my pants?" Ritter asked.

"I'll laugh at you," Christian said.

Ritter shot him a look. Before he could respond, a group of Marauders wearing masks exited the building. They stopped in front of Christian and removed their masks. Emil, Fluse, and Lage were among them.

"You're okay," Emil said between gasps.

Christian nodded.

"And you have Ritter," Fluse said, his hands on his knees.

"Serpent was trying to kill him," Christian said. "He failed."

"You killed him?" Emil asked.

"I had no choice," Christian said. "He literally had Ritter by the throat. Where did the Smoke come from? Did Serpent have it?"

"I think it was Grundig," Fluse said. "He had some."

Emil's eyes widened in shock. "He did? And you knew?"

"I saw it this morning for the first time," Fluse said. "I thought he was securing it in case they broke in. But I had no idea he'd do this."

"The smoke is starting to clear," Lage said, pointing toward the windows. Only a few faint wisps of the toxic gas were still escaping.

The door nearest the lab flew open then, and more Marauders poured out. Emil and Christian ran over to meet them. They pulled off their masks and went through the familiar ritual of coughing, gasping, and leaning on their knees.

"Where's Grundig?" Emil asked.

Two of the Marauders looked up and shook their heads in unison.

THE MARAUDERS' HEADQUARTERS,
PARIS FRANCE

Christian didn't need field glasses or a scope to see the blood mixed in with the residue from the tear gas. It was easy to spot, even from the third-floor window from where he'd spilled it. He could admire his handiwork from up there.

It had been a wasted effort. The Maîtres Rouges had still breached the compound, and Grundig had still released the Smoke and killed nearly thirty men in total, including several Marauders.

Christian and the others had found Grundig's body in his lab, covered in jet-black sediment from the Smoke. The stench of Benzin and black tar was still hanging over all the halls of the factory a day later, forcing the cleanup crew to wear gas masks.

Why? Why had Grundig unleashed the Smoke? Had he been afraid of being killed by the gang? Had he preferred this kind of death over a beating? Or had he decided that if they were going to get him, he would take as many people with him as possible?

The Panzer was clear of residue and blood, so it lumbered away from the gate and crawled out of view like a timid street dog. Three Marauders armed with rifles stepped in front of the broken entrance, prepared to challenge anyone trying to enter the compound. The Maîtres Rouges had been defeated, but that didn't mean Paris was safe.

There would always be another Serpent, or another Wegener.

Christian brought his scope up to his eye and inspected the guards. During yesterday's attack, he'd shot five Maîtres where those guards were standing now. Three of the gang members had been on top of the Panzer. One had made it to the ground. The other had fallen halfway through the shattered gate. His fellow Maîtres Rouges had lifted him out of the opening, tossed him aside, and continued their attack.

So they could die from inhaling German Black Smoke.

Christian aimed the rifle toward the center of the compound. He'd shot another five Maîtres there. Or had it been ten? How many times had he reloaded? How many shots had he fired? How many had found their targets?

Too late to count now. The bodies were gone. Had anyone come to claim them? Sisters? Wives? How did you report a missing family member in a city that had no government? Could you accuse someone of murder in a city that had no laws?

Was Serpent guilty of anything? Or had he simply lost a battle in a new world where the strongest ones ruled? Did the Marauders own the city now?

They'd lost a third of their men yesterday. Most of those losses had come after Serpent's men had broken in via the back of the factory, but a handful more had perished when Grundig had unleashed his Smoke.

Why?

Christian stood and pointed the rifle down, replaying the sharp angle he'd taken when he'd emptied his weapon for the last time.

Thirteen. He'd shot at least thirteen men from this window. He'd tried to avoid killing, even started out shooting only to wound instead of kill. But he'd racked up his highest body count ever.

"There you are," said Lage from behind him.

Christian jumped and swung the rifle around.

"Whoa!" Lage said with his hands up. "It's just me."

That would have made Christian's count fourteen. No, seventeen. He had killed two people in the hallway, and then Serpent.

"The monseigneur will be here soon," Lage went on. "Zimmerman wants you to be there when they talk to him."

Christian shrugged and walked to the window that looked out the back of the factory. He could have taken out at least five more Maîtres, maybe ten of them, from this side. Twenty-seven in one day? That had to be worth some kind of award.

Charlotte's words came back to Christian then: *You decide when you are done.*

"Are you coming?" Lage asked.

"No," Christian said without looking up from the shattered back gate.

"But Zimmerman asked for you. They need you, especially since we're short—"

"Short an officer? Or short thirty men? We're done, Lage. We're finished. It's over. We defeated the Maîtres Rouges, but there's no way we can defend this city. No way we can defend *ourselves.*"

"Wh-what? What do you mean?"

"I don't know."

"Look. We're all upset over Grundig—"

"*Upset?*" Christian crossed his arms without looking away from the window. "I'm not upset, Lage. *Upset* is a word for polite company. For men like the monseigneur. I'm *furious.* I'm furious that Grundig killed himself. I'm furious that we had to lose a third of our men fighting *people* instead of the aliens that are supposed to be the real threat."

Lage stepped to Christian's side to catch his eye. The younger soldier was shaking, but it was hard for Christian to tell if it was from fear or anger. "You're furious?" Lage hissed. "So you're going to quit? That's your answer?"

Now that Lage had said it out loud, it was clear. Christian

was done. He wasn't sure if humanity was worth saving from the aliens, but if it was, he wasn't the man to do it. With Grundig and his toys gone, Christian was more proficient at killing than anyone else left in the Marauders.

What kind of savior did that make him?

"Yes, that's my answer," Christian said.

"I thought you were different," Lage said.

The words hit Christian so hard that he had to lean on the window to steady himself.

I thought you were different. He'd said the same thing to Emil in Reims. Emil had been ready to give up on fighting Wegener and head home, and Christian had accused him of being like every other officer.

But this was different. Wasn't it?

Emil hadn't racked up a deadly body count in Reims like Christian had yesterday, and things then had been nowhere near as desperate as they were right now. Most of all, Christian was not Emil Zimmerman. Emil had been their leader back then, even if he'd refused to admit it. Christian was nothing more than the designated assassin.

"Different?" Christian repeated, and turned to make eye contact with the younger soldier.

"From Fluse and Zimmerman," Lage said. "They want to talk, and plan, and think. Not you. You act. You're ready to do what it takes. Or, at least you were."

Lage was talking about shooting those ravageurs in Goussainville. Stealing the Panzer. Lage had been watching him, even back then. Taking notes. Learning exactly the wrong things.

Christian sighed.

"What?" Lage asked. "What's wrong with that?"

The compound's back entrance had two armed guards. The surrounding area was already clear. No blood stains there. Emil hadn't killed anyone. Did that make him less of a soldier than Christian? Or a better man?

"You think I'm better than them because I act without thinking?" Christian asked. "Without making plans?"

"That's not what I meant," Lage said.

Christian shifted his weight against one arm, keeping his eyes on the back gate. A single soldier walked out of the building with planks balanced on one shoulder. He set them down and walked back.

"You . . . act," Lage tried again. "You do what needs to be done. You're not afraid of getting your hands dirty. You're the one who finally got Serpent! And how many of his men did you shoot from up here? Fifteen? Twenty?"

Mein Gott. Did Lage want to be a killer, just like Christian?

"You lost family to the Martians?" Christian asked.

"Haven't we all?" Lage replied with a shrug.

This young soldier was yet another child consigned to a life of revenge. Just like Patty.

"So you want to kill Martians and anyone who works with them," Christian said.

"Don't you?" Lage asked.

"I thought I did," Christian said wistfully.

The other Marauder walked back outside with a toolbox in his hands. He set it down and pulled out a hammer and a box of nails.

"And now you don't?" Lage growled. "After all this, you want to work with them, too?"

"Are those my only choices? Kill them or join them? I want people to be safe. Does that mean the Martians have to die? I hope not, because I'm not sure we can kill them all."

But quitting wouldn't make it happen, either. Would it?

The other Marauder laid out the planks in a neat row, then stepped back and eyed them. He was going to fix the back gate. It was a big job, probably too big for one man.

But he was trying.

"Let's go talk to the monseigneur," Christian said.

CHAPTER 32

THE MARAUDERS' HEADQUARTERS, PARIS, FRANCE

Ritter sat up and straightened his shirt collar while eyeing Emil and Christian contemptuously. He leaned forward as he massaged his wrists, smoothed his pants, then exhaled. "I told you I wasn't going anywhere," he said.

"Tying you up while we cleaned up your mess made sure of that," Christian said. "We'll take you back down to your cell as soon as we're finished."

"*My* mess?" Ritter exclaimed.

"Serpent was here to kill you. And you're welcome, by the way. I quite literally saved your life."

Ritter turned away. He was a pompous, arrogant, self-centered coward who couldn't bring himself to thank Christian. It just wasn't in him to do it, Christian guessed.

"He'll thank us by telling us more about his former friends," Emil said.

Ritter sniffed and crossed his arms.

"No? Okay. Bye." Emil stood up and opened the door to Ritter's room.

"What?" Ritter said.

"I said goodbye," Emil said. "Get out."

"I can leave?" Ritter asked, raising an eyebrow.

"Yes. Absolutely. You have no value to me as a prisoner anymore. Leave."

Ritter stood and took a step toward the door.

"And say hello to Serpent's friends for me," Emil went on. "They'll find you."

Ritter snorted as he approached the door.

"After I send word that I've released you, of course," Emil added.

Ritter stopped and spun around to face Emil. "You wouldn't," Ritter said.

"I already wrote the message. Auf Wiedersehen, Ritter."

Ritter remained frozen in place.

"Get out," Emil said as he waved his hands to herd Ritter out of the room. "I don't need you, and I'm certainly not going to shelter and feed you."

"But they'll kill me."

"Not my problem, collaborator. Guards!"

Two armed men entered from either side of the door.

"Show him out of the compound," Emil instructed.

The guards grabbed Ritter by the shoulders and dragged him toward the open door.

"Get your hands off me," Ritter continued as he disappeared out the door and around the corner with the guards. "You can't do this. I'm a Hauptmann in the German Army. I'll have you up on charges . . ."

Emil crossed his arms and looked at his watch before smiling at Christian.

"Wait!" Ritter's voice echoed from down the hall. "Wait! I can help you! I can tell you how to find the Martians!"

"Bring him back!" Emil bellowed as he poked his head out the door.

Ritter appeared in the doorway again, walking on his own this time. Emil nodded to the guards, and they closed the door behind Ritter, who walked back to his chair.

"Please, take a seat," Emil quipped. "And start talking. Quickly."

Ritter smoothed his pants and straightened his cuffs again. But instead of his earlier contemptuous look, he looked like a little boy with his hand stuck in a cookie jar. "Well, they didn't exactly reveal all of their plans to me."

Emil turned toward the door and opened his mouth to shout. Christian could tell he was enjoying himself.

"Wait!" Ritter said. "I do have an idea."

"We don't want 'ideas,'" Christian said. "We want to know what the aliens are planning and how to stop them. *Your* decision to deal with Serpent cost us a lot. Now it's time to pay." He crossed his arms and leaned in toward Ritter.

"The Martians have to eat," Ritter said.

"Of course they do," Christian said. "Is this your penetrating insight?"

"You don't understand. They have to eat *us*." Ritter pointed at Christian, then at Emil, and then at himself.

"That's not exactly a secret, Ritter," Emil said.

"They don't do well on anything else. They need people."

Christian held up his hands. "Then why do they keep leaving dead bodies behind? I've seen two sites in just the past few weeks where they've left plenty of scorched and broken bodies."

"They can't just grab someone and pop them in their mouths," Ritter said. "They need harvester machines and a bunch of other hardware to extract the blood."

"I remember that from the Englishman's book," Emil said.

What was Ritter trying to say? Was this some kind of diversion?

Christian took a seat. "I've heard about them, too," he said. "They had one in Karlsruhe during the first invasion. But I didn't see one out by the ravageur—your—compound."

"Of course not," Ritter said. "They weren't going to do it in front of us. They changed shifts to go eat every twelve hours or so."

Christian thought back to the scare he'd had with Otto the first time he'd visited Ritter's camp. "Ah. I saw that," he said.

"They're still doing that?" Ritter asked. "Even after they leveled the place?"

"No. But they were doing it when I sat by one of your armored cars and watched your men get drunk." Christian offered a mirthless grin. "I sat on your perimeter while your idiot guards lit three cigarettes on one match."

Ritter laughed. "They were lucky to be alive doing that in front of you."

He'd probably meant it as a compliment, but it didn't sting Christian any less.

"So what you're saying is, there must be a feeding center somewhere near your camp," Emil said.

"I know there was one northeast of there," Ritter said. "I'm not sure how far, probably within a few kilometers. We always had the same Wanderers at our camp. You start to recognize them after a while. But I wouldn't be surprised if they built a new one closer to here to prepare for the attack."

"But that means they need people to fill it," Emil said.

Christian's stomach dropped to his knees.

"Of course," Ritter said. "There's a method to how they decide which villages they take people from and which ones they leave alone for later. And they rarely wipe an entire town out, unless it's very small or they need to stock up."

Stock up?

"If they're finally massing for an attack on Paris," Ritter went on, "I wouldn't want to live in any of the villages around here."

Like Goussainville.

CHAPTER 33
OPEN COUNTRY, NORTH OF PARIS

"This is the fourth pair of Wanderers we've seen cross here in ninety minutes," Emil said to Christian, looking north through his field glasses.

They were about forty kilometers due north of Paris in open country, outside the range of their normal scouting and supply missions. The consequences of the kaiser's war and the second Martian invasion were painfully apparent this far outside the city. On their ride out yesterday, Christian had noticed abandoned farmsteads and even a burned-out village.

This morning had greeted him and the others with two blackened human skeletons guarding a barn about three klicks past their camp. Ritter had lost his breakfast at the sight, and Emil had been too deeply affected by it to mock him.

"Yeah, we're on to something," Christian replied as he surveyed the area with his rifle scope. The field stood on the far side of a stand of trees that was just a little too thin to call woods. The Wanderers were nearly out of sight, but they were headed the same way as the previous groups. "Good job, Ritter. Do we scout ahead, Emil? Or take the whole group?"

As soon as the ramifications of what Ritter had told them back at headquarters had become clear, so had the Marauders' only path to victory: find the Martian feeding grounds, and destroy them before the aliens could "stock up," as Ritter had put it.

Emil had wanted to split up their forces to avoid leaving Paris undefended. But Christian and Fluse had both pushed for them to take every man and weapon, arguing that if they failed, the state they left in Paris wouldn't make a difference. Eventually, they agreed to leave a small skeleton crew behind. Now, they were traveling with five Panzers, eight carts—four of which were mounted with heat rays, the rest to help transport any people they managed to rescue—and thirty men, including Ritter.

"Scout," Emil said. "The element of surprise might be our only hope. We'll take you with us, Ritter."

Ritter, who was sitting in the back of the cart Emil and Christian were sharing, sniffed.

"You trust him?" Christian said.

Ritter leered at him.

"Of course not," Emil said. "But I trust him less with Fluse, who would need to divide his attention between minding him and running the convoy. And who knows? He might accidentally say something useful again."

"Very amusing, Zimmerman," Ritter grumbled.

"I thought so," said Emil.

Moments later, Christian and Emil spoke to Fluse, who directed the group to camouflage the vehicles and settle in. Meanwhile, Emil grabbed the extra horses they'd taken for scouting: two riding horses from the city stable that worked with the Resistance, and an aging draft horse donated to the cause by the man who'd shown Christian the catacombs.

"You don't expect me to ride *that*," Ritter said, curling his lip at the larger horse.

"You can walk if you want, but I think you'll get tired," Emil said.

"I'm a cavalry captain," Ritter said.

"Then you're the best man to get that horse to move," said Christian.

Emil winked at him.

The Wanderers had continued north by northwest from where the convoy was stopped. It was away from Goussainville, where Christian wanted to go. He knew that leading the convoy there could attract the aliens, but he couldn't help but wonder if Charlotte, Patty, and Francois were still safe.

Had he guided them into danger once again?

Christian rode in parallel with Emil and Ritter for a few kilometers before any Wanderers came into view again. Three, this time. But they dropped out of sight soon after the men spotted them.

"If we follow them, we're sitting ducks," Ritter said.

Emil nodded and led them east, skirting the ridgeline and flanking the aliens. After a few hundred meters, they reached a stand of trees.

"We'll leave the horses here and take a look," Emil said.

The trees skirted the ridgeline, giving them a perfect view of what turned out to be more of a hollow than a valley. What was lying inside that hollow made Christian gasp.

It was the tenth circle of Hell.

Cages overflowing with people sat at one end of the Martian camp. It was clear, even from a distance, that many of the humans had been there for days. They were lying in their own filth, soiled enough that Christian wasn't sure if he was sensing or imagining the stench. Some who lay on the cage floors looked dead, exhausted, or simply despondent. Others clenched the cages' steel bars with white-knuckled fists.

Infernal machines, as tall as barns and as long as train cars, stood adjacent to the cages. They were still at the moment, but it wasn't hard to imagine what they were for. Everyone had read the book Emil had mentioned back at headquarters; it had been translated into German within a year of its release. The Martians used devices to bleed out their prey because they had no digestive systems of their own.

"It's an abomination," Emil said.

"Yes,' Ritter said. "And it's clustered right here, all in one place. One swift blow, and we hurt them. Badly."

"*We?*" Christian asked, raising an eyebrow.

"Since you ruined *my* plans, I might as well throw in with yours," Ritter said. "I'm dead by the end of the day either way. At least I'll die a soldier who tried to save his people."

He smiled—which was not at all a comforting sight to Christian—and turned to walk to his horse.

"But what about their prisoners?" Emil asked.

Ritter stopped and turned to face Emil and Christian. "They're dead either way, too," he said. "A few might escape, but then we'd have to figure out how to carry them back to Paris."

Christian figured there had to be at least a hundred people in those cages—maybe even more that he couldn't see from his vantage point. Just when it seemed like he might have some principles, Ritter was writing them all off as dead.

"No," Christian said. "I don't accept that."

"Then how do you propose to save them?" Ritter asked. "Do you want to run down there, unlock their cages, and escort them out before the Martians notice?"

"That brings up a good point," Emil said. "How are we going to move four Panzers over here without alerting them?"

"We're not going to," Ritter said with a chuckle. "You know how sensitive their hearing is. At some point, they'll hear the Panzers and counterattack. You need to get as close to this mess as quickly as you can. Strike quickly, like lightning."

"That sounds like a great way to get the Panzers surrounded," Christian said.

Ritter crossed his arms. He opened his mouth to speak, but Emil cut him off.

"Charging into a group of light infantry or an enemy camp

on horseback might make sense, Ritter. But you're talking about driving four Panzers into a group of . . ." Emil paused and counted them under his breath. "Fifteen Wanderers. It would be a bloodbath."

"I guess armored vehicles aren't cavalry. But what does that have to do with the prisoners?"

Christian already had an idea of what Emil was going to suggest. He took his rifle off his shoulder and examined the cages with his scope. "Looks like some kind of electronic mechanism," he said. "Might open if I put a few rounds through them."

"If they don't, we can't help those people unless we can drive out all the aliens and take time to figure out how to open them," Emil said.

"So you're going to leave him here, and he'll try to free the prisoners while the Panzers attack," Ritter said.

"Outstanding!" Emil said. "You're not so bad at strategy after all."

Ritter stared into the distance for a full minute, his arms still crossed. "I'm not so bad a shot myself, and there are at least a few more cages beyond that one," he eventually said. "I'll stay here."

Christian threw up his hands in surprise. "You were ready to let them die a moment ago. And now you're ready to sacrifice yourself to save them?"

"Sacrifice myself? I never said that. I'm going to succeed."

CHAPTER 34

OPEN COUNTRY, NORTH OF PARIS

"You know we're going to have to get closer," Ritter said about an hour after Emil had left to retrieve the Panzers and start the attack. "There's no way an M98 round is going to split those locks in a single shot."

"Depends on the quality of the lock," Christian said. "We don't know where those cages are from or what they're made of."

"An optimist."

By then, Ritter and Christian had finished scouting the perimeter of the Martians' feeding ground. There were six cages sitting at one end of the hollow. Three feeding machines sat in the middle, and the last third was open space for the Wanderers to rest and communicate. The camp was nearly silent, but from the information that had been gathered after the first Martian Attack, Christian knew that Wanderers could communicate with frequencies inaudible to human hearing.

"They're going to eat soon," Ritter said.

"A pessimist."

Ritter shrugged, turned, and climbed onto his horse. "It's probably time to take our positions," he said, and rode away. He would start at the far end, armed with his pistol and Emil's rifle.

Christian had been nervous at the idea of giving Ritter weapons, but Emil had insisted that Ritter was more of a pragmatist than a traitor.

Christian walked back to the spot he had chosen. It gave him a clear line of sight at two of his three cage doors. He raised the rifle again, checked the angle, let the light breeze from the west brush his cheek, and rehearsed his shots.

For the first time since he had been conscripted into the army, he was using his skill with the rifle to save lives rather than take them.

The sides of the hollow had a gentle slope, with young trees and small bushes that would give Christian decent—though less than perfect—cover if he had to move in closer.

A crack that cut through to his gut like nearby thunder sounded from the direction of the Panzers. Seconds later, the distant hooting of a distressed Wanderer echoed from the same way.

The battle was on.

Eight of the Wanderers rushed out of the resting area, leaving seven behind. Whatever the call for help had communicated must have been dire. Hopefully, that was a good sign.

Christian shifted in place and checked his shot again. He raised the scope and checked the far side of the hollow, but Ritter was out of sight.

Three more hoots echoed off in the distance. The third was high-pitched and sustained. Three more Wanderers left the hollow, as a tremendous explosion echoed from the same direction as the calls for help, and two more followed it.

Two Wanderers left. Time to go.

Christian squeezed off his first shot, striking the lock mechanism on the first cage. One prisoner jumped in response. A woman screamed.

No. The last thing Christian wanted to do was draw the Martian's attention.

Another prisoner, a man in what might have been a soiled

uniform, gestured to her, and she fell silent. No response from the remaining Wanderers followed.

Three shots sounded from the far side of the hollow. Hopefully, Ritter was hitting locks and not people.

Christian resumed his work. He pulled. Pushed. Aimed. Exhaled. Squeezed. Pulled. Pushed.

Smoke rose from the lock this time, but it held fast. He scrambled down the slope, hearing Ritter's continuing fire as he reached a spot roughly halfway down the ridge and began again.

Christian aimed. Exhaled. Squeezed. Pulled. Pushed.

Another wisp of smoke as the cage door swung open. Success!

There was no time to celebrate as a deafening howl rose from inside the hollow. Both Wanderers had sprung to life.

Christian ran wide around the perimeter to give himself clear sight to the next cage while getting farther away from the Wanderers. One of them loomed over the cages as the hum of an energizing heat ray vibrated in Christian's chest. But it didn't fire yet. Was it being cautious?

Or, maybe it didn't want to kill its lunch.

Christian aimed. Exhaled. Squeezed. Pulled. Pushed. And then ran.

The ray nearly signed Christian's heels as he ran closer to the cages, forcing the Martians to risk killing their prisoners if he fired again.

Christian aimed. Squeezed. Pulled. Pushed. Ran again.

Missed by at least a meter. Damn scope was in the way. Christian reminded himself to breathe.

Another run, this time on a sharp angle that kept the lock in sight and the prisoners nearby.

Christian aimed. Breathed.

A heat ray throbbed, loud enough that it was right on top of Christian.

He ran again, rolling quickly enough to see a narrow green

beam strike right where he'd been. How had the Martian made that shot with its poor vision?

The ray sounded again. Christian ran toward the alien this time, only stopping when he reached its limbs. A Martian Wanderer could never find its own feet.

Shouts and screams sounded from the far end of the hollow. The other Wanderer was close to the cages. It brandished its aiming mirror toward the furthest corner of the hollow and started to energize.

The mirror! Of course.

He aimed. Squeezed. Pulled. Pushed.

The mirror shattered as the gut-wrenching tone of the heat ray continued. But rather than power down, the Martian's arm exploded, throwing the craft across one of the food processing machines in a flurry of high-pitched hoots and flailing tentacles.

Christian stared, transfixed. Finally, the sound of human voices shouting pulled him back to where he stood.

The prisoners! They were shouting and pointing.

He ran instinctively as another blast from the other Wanderer missed with its narrow beam. This time, he headed directly for the cage, raising the rifle as he approached. Only a fool would try a shot like this on the run.

But only a fool would run into a duel with a Wanderer.

Christian squeezed off the shot, stopping just long enough to take aim. Smoke billowed from the mechanism, but it held fast.

But no response from the Wanderer. Christian was too close to the cage to risk incinerating the prisoners. Might as well try again.

He pulled. Pushed. Exhaled. Aimed. Squeezed. Pulled. Pushed.

The door swung open, and as the prisoners flooded out, the telltale hum of the remaining Wanderer's heat ray resonated in Christian's chest.

He was enough of a threat for the Martians to risk killing some of the prisoners now.

He bounded off for the next cage, determined to free the humans inside despite what might happen to him. The throbbing of the energizing heat ray continued as the Wanderer trudged after him.

Christian dove for cover, rolling to face the Wanderer as he landed. He raised his rifle to fire—

And a weapon fired from behind him. The drone of the heat ray ceased, and the Wanderer howled. Its aiming mirror was gone.

"Stop staring, and take care of that last cage!" Ritter shouted.

Christian spun around with his rifle still raised and put a round into the lock. Smoke rose from it.

He pulled. Pushed. Aimed.

"Look out!" Ritter yelled.

Christian was hurled onto his side, and something inside him cracked as he hit the ground. Everything briefly went black. As he came to, he felt a sharp burning sensation in his side as he inhaled. A broken rib, no doubt.

"Get up!" Ritter shouted from a different direction.

Christian scrambled to his feet and lunged forward just as a Wanderer's foot struck the ground behind him. He hurried forward, straining to hold his rifle and his aching side at the same time.

"Here!" Ritter shouted as he rode to Christian with a hand outstretched.

Christian dropped the rifle, took the hand, and grimaced in pain as he jumped onto the moving horse, sprawled across its back as it ran away from the Wanderer.

The Wanderer howled in frustration and thundered after them.

Nearly passing out from pain, Christian strained to spin around and sit on the back of the horse, his hands grasping Ritter's waist.

"Hold on!" Ritter shouted before riding in a serpentine pattern, circumnavigating the massive machines in the center of the hollow. Only a skilled rider like him could coax a horse better suited for pulling a plow into moving with such speed and agility. But the Wanderer charged after them at a frightfully rapid pace, gaining a few meters on them between twists and turns. Christian's vision dimmed from pain as he held on for dear life.

Ritter tacked toward the entrance ramp, but the Wanderer must have seen through the ruse, because it moved to block them.

"Verdammt!" Ritter said as he drew the horse to a stop. The Wanderer froze, too, waiting for Ritter to make a move.

A howl rose behind them then. The other Wanderer was back on its feet.

"Well, let's see if this horse is fast enough to make it through its legs," Ritter said. "Either that, or we split up, and maybe one of us will make it."

"I can't run," Christian said. "It'll get me first."

"Exactly," said Ritter.

The deep hum of several heat rays warming up in unison cut Ritter off. The Wanderer near them staggered forward as three rays hit it. Two others fired over the men's heads to strike the Wanderer behind it.

The Panzers had arrived.

Within seconds, the two Wanderers in the hollow were down in a haze of heat rays and hoots. Christian slid off the horse and dropped to the ground. Ritter jumped off after him.

"I guess that Arschloch broke a couple of your ribs?" Ritter asked.

Christian nodded with a grimace.

"Here, I have a medical kit," Ritter said, pulling a flask from a pouch on his saddle.

Christian opened the container and took a long drink. Peppermint schnaps. Not his favorite, but he'd take any port in this storm.

He passed out after the third sip.

CHAPTER 35

THE MARAUDERS' HEADQUARTERS, PARIS, FRANCE

Christian cracked one eye open, then another. He blinked at the bright sunlight and regretted, not for the first time, taking a room on the eastern side of the factory building. It was 08:30. Might as well get dressed and grab some breakfast in the mess hall before the morning's food ran out, or before service ended in advance of lunch.

Other than some looting by Serpent's gang, the kitchen had withstood the invasion by the Maîtres Rouges rather well. So well that the Marauders were feeding most of the prisoners they had freed up north four days ago.

But the headquarters still bore the scars of the attack. Christian walked past burnt and broken walls and had to detour to the far corner of the building to avoid a collapsed stairwell.

Every step through headquarters brought Grundig to mind. The Marauders had decimated the Martian's capability to feed themselves, freed more than a hundred prisoners, and taken on seven more Wanderers on their way back from the mission.

But it was still too late for Grundig.

It wasn't too late for Charlotte and her family, though.

Christian's ribs were sore, and the ride would be hard, but he would be heading to Goussainville today. He'd been resting for a few days and didn't want to wait any longer.

"Good to see you up and about," Emil said as Christian reached the table in the mess hall that he was sharing with Fluse, Ritter, and a few other men.

Ritter had proven trustworthy, if not necessarily loyal, at the Martian feeding ground. He'd even been helping with planning missions to find and destroy more of them.

"How are you feeling?" Fluse asked.

"Better," Christian said with a smile. "Much better." He set down his mug of coffee and a plate of eggs and bacon, then took a seat. "How's it going with the missions?"

Four groups, each with two horse-drawn carts and ample explosives, had been sent out of Paris in the cardinal directions. These were risky missions, since the carts wouldn't have the power of the entire fleet of Panzers behind them. But the Marauders knew what to expect. The plan was to wire the explosives with timers set to ignite after quietly opening the cages and leading the prisoners to safety.

If the Marauders in each cart didn't think that was possible, they had orders to return and retrieve a better-fortified team.

"We've wiped out three feeding grounds so far," Emil said before picking up his coffee cup and standing. "Hopefully, at least one more group will return today." He walked over to the coffeepot to get a refill.

"Maybe one of us should have gone with them," Christian said, not really meaning it. He had almost been relieved to be too injured to be considered for the missions.

"Bad idea," Ritter said. "The aliens are going to be here looking for food. But I'm sure they could have used your rifle."

It had felt wonderful to use that rifle to save lives instead of take them, especially after the Maîtres Rouges' attack on headquarters. But that didn't mean Christian was in a hurry to return to combat yet.

"Actually, I'm headed to Goussainville today," Christian said.

Emil sat down and raised an eyebrow. "You feel up to the ride?"

"I think so. And I want to check in on our friends up there." Christian scooped up a forkful of eggs, realizing that with the soreness of the ribs finally subsiding, his appetite had returned with a vengeance.

"We got word yesterday that the area around Goussainville has been quiet," Fluse said. "Is there anyone specific you want to check on?" At that question, he grinned.

"I don't know if we can afford to lose you if the Martians attack," Ritter said.

"I'm only one man," Christian said, heat rising to his face. "And Charlotte and her family are up there because we—I uprooted them from their home."

"To be fair, they'd be in at least as much danger if you never sought her out," Fluse said.

"I don't know what the hell you two idiots are talking about," Ritter said. "But we don't have time to worry about one family when the entire city of Paris—the largest and most populated city in the country—is in danger of attack. And you're not just one man, Beckenbauer. You're one of the few men we have who can disable a Wanderer with an M98."

"You made the same shot," Christian said. "And it's a trick I learned from Emil."

"That's a great point," Emil said. "Christian here is our best sniper, and his ability to quickly take out an aiming mirror is almost uncanny. But instead of fretting over having enough heat rays and armor, we should put sharpshooters alongside the triggers for the radioflashes."

Ritter nodded with a frown. "Not a bad idea."

"And I hate to lose your eye when the risk of an attack is so imminent, Christian," Emil added. "But you've earned it, and we could use a scout up in that area, too."

Christian breathed a sigh of relief.

"Can you be back tomorrow, just to be safe?" Emil asked.

"We heard back from Germany, and the message was mixed at best."

Christian raised an eyebrow as he took another bite of eggs.

"They found feeding grounds just west of Berlin and wiped them out, along with nearly a dozen Wanderers," Emil explained.

"Mixed?" Fluse pounded a fist on the tabletop. "That's fantastic news!"

"Berlin was under attack before the expeditionary force made it home," Emil said. "Another dozen Wanderers attacked with heat rays and cages to take prisoners."

The table fell silent as Christian considered this. What if the Martians were already doing that in the villages north of Paris?

On the ride to Goussainville, Christian clutched his side as he slowed the horse. His ribs hadn't healed enough for the ride, and he'd pay for it that night. He'd probably even pay for it for another couple of weeks after making it back to Paris. But he had to check on Charlotte and the other residents, even if he was only one man.

He guided the horse over the shallow drainage trench bordering the road, wincing as the horse hopped over the gap to a grassy field where it could graze. Then he eased himself off the horse and leaned against a tree to give his sore side a break. The trip to Goussainville was a short one without fully laden carts in tow, so he had plenty of time.

When the Martians had attacked Reims with six Wanderers, they'd decimated entire neighborhoods before the Marauders had ignited Grundig's radioflash. Now they'd marched on Berlin with twice that number. Emil had said the casualties were enormous, and the German Army had finally prevailed only because they'd received plans on how to build their own heat rays. Those plans had come from Grundig, and now he was gone. What would they do if the Martians countered with an even deadlier weapon?

As the horse grazed on the tall grass, it swung its tail lazily. It was only 11:00, and Christian idly wondered if he should find a shady spot and rest until after noon. But the other part of him wondered if the Martians were already on the move, menacing Goussainville while he wasted time.

He was halfway to his horse when he got his answer. A Wanderer howled as it lumbered into view, a cage under one tentacle and a heat ray in another.

The alien machine emerged from a stand of trees at the northern end of the grassy field. It moved rapidly on its spindly legs, using four of them to run at a frightful pace. That didn't give Christian enough time to mount his horse, especially with his sore ribs. He smacked the steed to startle it into running to safety, then took off on his own for the road and the cover of the woods on its opposite side.

He was halfway there when the horse screamed, but he only dared look after he'd reached cover. The horse was in the cage, with two of its legs protruding from the bottom of the steel prison. One of them dangled at an unnatural angle. Christian pulled his rifle from his shoulder, chambering a round as he brought the sight up to his eye.

He sighted the mirror. Exhaled. Squeezed the trigger.

The mirror shattered with a satisfying *pop*.

He pulled the bolt. Pushed it back to chamber.

His extra ammo was in the saddlebag, which was still on the horse. He had four rounds left in the rifle.

The horse screamed again.

Christian exhaled, then squeezed the trigger again.

The horse's screaming stopped.

The Wanderer howled and charged in Christian's direction. He turned and ran as fast as he could without passing out from the pain.

The Martians were on the attack; and he was stranded with four bullets, two cracked ribs, and no horse.

CHAPTER 36

THE SOUTHERN FACE OF THE THIERS WALL, PARIS, FRANCE

Zimmerman was a sentimental fool, if Ritter was honest. The city would be under attack within hours, and he'd let his second-in-command take furlough to check on some girl and her family. Worse, he was wasting time coordinating supply runs for refugees and taking a meeting with a woman who claimed she was a scientist, instead of shoring up his defenses.

But Zimmerman *was* a halfway decent strategist. Seeding the perimeter of the city with Grundig's radioflash devices meant they had a shot at defending the city when the Martians attacked. Posting sharpshooters at strategic chokepoints around the city was a brilliant way to compensate for his shortage of numbers.

Before taking the coward's way out, Grundig had devised a way to break civilian field glasses down into telescopes and mount them on rifles. They lacked the aiming reticle of a proper sniper's scope and looked ridiculous, but with practice the men could use them to make some impressive shots. That would give them a chance at taking out the Martians' aiming mirrors before the aliens got too close.

Ritter had spent the morning going over maps with

Zimmerman and Fluse, who had somehow grown into an actual man, picking out the best locations for the sharpshooters. Now, Ritter was taking a crew to one of those spots, the southwestern section of the Thiers wall.

The Thiers wall had been erected around the city about seventy years earlier. The Martians had damaged it during the first Attack, prompting the French to reinforce and raise the existing walls. Now, the Thiers wall stood as high as ten meters at some points. Not high enough for modern artillery or a determined Wanderer, but useful for snipers. It offered excellent line of sight and ample room for lateral movement.

It was the perfect spot for Ritter's sharpshooters.

His sharpshooters?

There he went again, thinking like he was a Marauder. Zimmerman and his Marauders were a means to an end, and nothing more. Ritter was only there because Zimmerman might give him an in with Central Command in Berlin. Hell, it had been little more than a week since he'd sent an assassin to shoot the man. With any luck, the Martians would attack from the north or east, and Ritter come out smelling like a rose regardless of how things went.

Ritter's section of the wall ended at the Seine and overlooked a sleepy village called Issy to the south. Issy housed enough people that it was a good target for hungry Martians, so in addition to the sniper coverage, a radioflash was buried near its southern border. Zimmerman had a Resistance member in the village with the trigger and instructions to hold off on firing the device until Ritter's flare flew overhead.

Ritter had his men spread out about twenty meters apart along the wall. Each man was armed with one of Grundig's makeshift scopes, and a lucky few also had spotters with field glasses. The last man was in position on a parapet on the southeastern corner of the wall near the bank of the Seine. He was more of a boy than a man, but he had a reputation for being a steady shot. His position overlooked a patch of woods that sat between Issy and the Seine.

"Once you fire, start moving!" Ritter shouted to the men. "Even if you hit the Wanderer you're gunning for, one of the others might ignite this rotting wood canopy in seconds." He pointed at the boy to make his point. "It's a wonder this wall is still standing. Verdammt French don't take care of anything but cheese wheels and wine glasses."

"Where do you recommend I focus my attention, sir?" the boy asked. "The river? Or the woods?"

To Ritter, the obvious answer would have been "Both!", followed by him smacking the boy across the back of his head. But now was the time for confidence, not correction.

"If I had to lay odds, I'd expect them to come from the woods," Ritter said as he raised his field glasses and scanned the trees. "But that's just my gut talking. They might divide their forces and strike us from—"

A tiny flash of light grabbed Ritter's eye. It was a reflection from something in the trees about five degrees southwest.

"Scheiße," he cursed.

"Sir?" the boy said, sweat already collecting on his brow.

"They're out there," Ritter said. "But what are they waiting for?"

The boy raised his rifle and directed it where Ritter was looking, his finger on the trigger.

"What are you doing?" Ritter ordered. "That's a kilometer from here, probably a little more. You'll do nothing more than—"

The report of nearby rifle shots cut Ritter off. His heart climbed into his throat.

"Cease fire!" he bellowed, knowing it was already too late. "Cease fire!"

Three. Five. Eight. At least ten Wanderers burst through the tree line and started for the wall. Two more were working their way up the Seine.

Ritter ran toward the middle of his position where the flare, a rocket mounted on a pole, stood. He was still moving at a full sprint when he grabbed the string that would launch it high in the sky over Issy. He stumbled and fell as sparks from the flint spilled onto his jacket.

Five seconds passed.

Ritter stood and peered through the field glasses. A dozen Wanderers had emerged from the woods on the other side of Issy and were closing in on the village.

Ten seconds.

The first Wanderer that Ritter had spotted was alongside the village and headed for the wall.

Twenty seconds.

Six more Wanderers had reached the edge of Issy.

Thirty verdammt seconds.

Where the hell was that fool with the trigger?

A flash by the woods nearly blinded Ritter. He squeezed his eyes shut and shook his head, hoping to drive the spots in his vision away. The report reached his ears a second later.

When he could check with the field glasses again, he discovered that seven Wanderers had dropped to the ground. At least five were still on their way, and the idiot snipers were emptying their rifles at them.

"Stop it, you idiots!" Ritter snarled. "I don't want you to fire until you can see yourself in their aiming mirrors, got me?" He headed down the wall to coach the rest of the soldiers and resist the urge to strangle the Scheißkopf who fired first.

The Wanderers were closing on Paris fast now, ignoring Issy and focusing their wrath on the men on the wall. Two of them had their aiming mirrors shot out within a minute of being within range. The other Wanderers, however, kept their mirrors out of sight. They couldn't fire at the men, but all the men could do was bounce rounds off the Martian armor, which they seemed more than happy to waste ammunition doing.

The first three Wanderers to reach the wall simply stepped

over it. The next two slowed down to have some fun. They scooped men up and hurled them into the city over back toward the woods.

Ritter scrambled down off the wall and mounted his horse. His line was breached, and his men were dead or fleeing for their lives. The path to the east was clear; and he had Alger, his cavalry horse, this time. He would be as far as Reims by nightfall and over the border tomorrow. He might even find a group of men to join there, or ride right to Berlin and plead his case with command.

A Wanderer extended a tentacle toward Ritter. He grabbed the reins and urged the horse away.

Until he noticed the tentacle had a mirror on it.

He unsheathed his pistol. Shooting from a moving horse wasn't difficult. It was damn near impossible. It was hard enough to hit a target while sitting still; doing it from a moving horse required skill, patience, and unnatural luck. The shot he'd made to save Beckenbauer had been one in a million, and it had been his fourth try. He might have neglected to mention that afterward.

Ritter aimed the pistol and squeezed off a shot. Not even close.

The rumbling started as he pulled the horse into a forty-five-degree turn, holding up the pistol like a circus performer struggling to keep his balance on a tight rope. He aimed and fired again.

The mirror shattered, but half remained in the frame on the Wanderer's tentacle.

Ritter shoved the pistol into his waistband, grabbed the reins with both hands, and spurred the horse west, toward the Seine and into the city. His thighs squeezed the spools of rope he'd hung on Alger's saddle. Those spools just might come in handy later.

As much as it pained Ritter to admit it, he couldn't leave Zimmerman to fight the aliens alone.

He turned again and urged Alger back into the fray. A bone-rattling explosion knocked him off the horse and onto his side, where he lay dazed for a few seconds before rolling onto his back. He tried to sit up, and then the world went black.

Christian emerged out of the shade and into bright midday light. He'd lost the Wanderer in the trees a good twenty minutes ago, guessing correctly that it wasn't willing to drop its cage to continue chasing him into the old-growth forest.

His compass was back in his saddlebags, with his spare rounds of ammo, water, and maps; and with the sun high in the sky, he wasn't sure if he was heading in a more easterly or southerly direction. But he was standing at the edge of a vineyard, which might have meant west.

But no matter where Christian was, what he needed was a horse and directions.

He jogged past rows of vines, admiring the precision with which they were arranged over their trellises. There was an art to this kind of farming. A kind of loving care that the farmers back home never had.

Eventually, a barn came into sight, and Christian picked up his pace. One man was guiding a mule hauling a cart filled with fertilizer, while another man watched him. The observer, who must have been the vintner in charge, wore clean clothes and stood with his arms crossed and a sour look on his face. Two horses grazed on a small patch of grass alongside the building.

"Hello," Christian said to the vintner. "Please, I need help. I need to go to Paris." Then, remembering where he was, he switched to French. "Do you speak German?"

"No German," the vintner said in heavily accented but understandable German. "Get off my vignoble."

"Please. I need to warn Paris. Martians are heading that way."

"Go," the vintner said, pointing down a nearby road.

"Please! You don't understand. Martians are here! They are going to Paris. I need to warn them—"

"German soldiers worse than Martians," the vintner interrupted, crossing his arms. "Leave. Now." His mouth was set in a line, and the tension in his shoulders was visible. Clearly, the war the Martians had interrupted—the one between Germany and the rest of Europe—had touched him in one way or another.

But there was no time for this. Christian couldn't beat the aliens to the city, but he could still help defend it and deliver a warning to the Marauders before the chaos reached headquarters. But what now? Shoot the vintner with his last round? He didn't want to kill a man for being upset over a war and then steal his horse. What if Christian knocked him out and tied him up instead? That seemed too severe.

Maybe a bluff would work.

Christian checked to make sure the man guiding the cart was out of sight, then pulled the rifle off his shoulder and pointed it at the vintner. "Get in the barn," he growled.

The vintner's face fell in unison with his arms as they dropped to his side.

"Now!" Christian snarled. "And hands over your head."

The vintner marched to the barn with his hands raised and led Christian inside. Christian looked around for something to safely restrain the man with. A rope, probably from a hay bale, was lying on the dirt floor.

Then Christian spotted his salvation. A gift from God.

An automobile. A Mercedes, not unlike the one he'd seen Ritter's men using in Goussainville. But instead of being burdened with makeshift armor, it was a pristine convertible roadster. Christian could make excellent time to Paris in that thing.

He used the rope to tie the vintner's hands behind his back and then to a cross member on the barn wall. The vintner raised his voice in protest, but Christian silenced him by brandishing the rifle.

Christian had never driven an automobile before, but he'd piloted a tractor a few times back in Leimersheim. He poked his head into the car's driver's side window, identified the spark advance, and turned it back to safely crank the engine.

The car started on the first pull.

The vintner howled with rage as Christian put the Mercedes in gear and stalled it, since he'd neglected to release the parking brake. He hopped out of the car, cranked it again, and spotted someone running toward the barn. He got back in and released the brake.

This time, the wheels spun on the barn's dirt floor, covering the bellowing vintner with dust as it flew out of the barn and down the road in the direction the man had pointed.

Now Christian just had to find Paris.

CHAPTER 37
PARIS, FRANCE

*B*ump.

Ritter shifted away from the annoyance that had tried to interfere with his nap.

Bump.

Verdammt. Why couldn't they leave him alone? It was the middle of—

An attack. A Martian Attack.

Ritter opened his eyes and was greeted by a bulbous black nose. Alger's nose.

"Good boy," Ritter whispered to his horse.

A Wanderer was sprawled across the wall, with one of its tentacles shattered into pieces. It had tried to fire with a broken mirror and suffered the consequences, like the one at the feeding ground north of Paris.

Ritter struggled to his feet, bearing the weight of his impact on the ground and every one of his forty-five years. But there was no time for self-pity. He had to get to Zimmerman's headquarters and make sure they knew what was happening on the city's southern border.

The Wanderers were only a few hundred meters away, but their backs were turned as they ranged toward the center of

Paris. Two of them had cages under their arms, and they were "talking" to each other with their infernal horns. Ritter imagined what their conversation must have sounded like: *"What are you in the mood for today, Schatz? German pot roast? Or a French soup? We could melt some cheese over it the way you like!"*

He climbed onto Alger and urged him on, guiding him over the bridge and on an easterly path that would give the Martian food shoppers a wide berth. But they didn't make it far before three more Wanderers, all carrying cages, came into view.

None of them were using heat rays. Had they all been disabled by snipers? Or were the aliens more worried about preserving their food supply? They hadn't used their Black Smoke, either. They were here for the cuisine, Ritter realized, and not the conquest.

He crossed back to the other shore, turned onto the avenue, and urged Alger into a full gallop. The only way he'd make it to the Marauders' compound was to pass ahead of the group of Martians he'd left behind on the southern edge of town.

Ritter found himself leaning in as he rode, basking in the rush of a cavalry charge for the first time in what felt like years. He'd spent too much time playing war games with Wegener and spy for the Martians. He was born for this. Riding a well-bred steed. Riding fast.

Outpacing the invaders from the south wasn't going to happen, though. The avenue opened into a market square, where a Wanderer was treating a panicking crowd like a buffet at a society party. One of its tentacles reached ominously for a little girl, no older than nine or ten as she fled in Ritter's direction.

Ritter pointed Alger toward her and squeezed the horse's sides with his heels. The horse accelerated so hard that Ritter had to hunker down to stay in the saddle. They reached the child only seconds ahead of the Martian claw, and Ritter grabbed her by the collar of her blouse.

The Wanderer hooted with a sound that Ritter could only describe as angry.

The child was light, but Ritter didn't have a firm grip on her. He angled with his horse toward a crowd of people, bellowed for attention, and tossed her toward them. Better some cuts and scrapes than an alien feeding machine.

Something brushed his leg. A tentacle! The Martian had stopped gathering people and was after him now.

Ritter narrowed his eyes. He wanted to see just how angry his new friend was.

He guided Alger away from the crowd, and the Wanderer followed him. Ritter took that as a good sign. Revenge was more important than lunch, then.

The Wanderer was unaccustomed to moving quickly on cobblestones, but it was clearly focused on taking its frustrations out on Ritter.

Ritter turned Alger around as soon as they were clear of the square. He unspooled one of his ropes, taking it into his hand just past the noose tied on the end and making sure it was completely clear of the saddle. An abandoned truck he'd spotted earlier was just what he needed.

Yes. That would do.

He guided Alger close to the vehicle and tossed the noose over a wheel. Then he pointed Alger's nose between the tentacles that served as the Wanderer's legs, letting the rope spool out behind him.

Alger was battle-hardened and trained; and while he'd never run down a Wanderer before, he was still up to the task. He snorted with anticipation as they reached the alien craft.

This was going to be the hard part, Ritter knew.

He tossed the other end of the rope, trying to catch it on the Wanderer's foot as it stepped over Ritter—and missed.

Verdammt.

Ritter pulled Alger to a stop, leaped from the saddle, picked up the rope, and remounted, ducking as another of the Wanderer's tentacles passed over his head. The alien vehicle was already on top of them, making it easy to toss the rope over a foot. Surviving that small victory was another issue entirely.

"Hut!" Ritter shouted as he spurred Alger back into action. "Hut, hut!"

Alger took off like a shot, with the Wanderer in hot pursuit.

Ritter had already been in the kaiser's army and the Hussars when the Martians had attacked the first time. He had enlisted only months earlier, with a commission awarded because of his father's position in the local government and his superior horsemanship. German artillery had kept the northern cities in the kaiser's young empire mostly safe, but the Martians had ravaged the countryside, wiping out entire villages and endangering the farms that fed the fatherland.

The Martians had turned out to be only days away from death, but the battles that the kaiser's mounted army had faced had lasted long enough to teach Ritter a few tricks, including this one.

He hoped this would still work.

Ritter spurred his horse on, not daring to look back—until he heard the groan of the truck's wheel and the satisfying crash of a Wanderer striking cobblestones.

Wanderers did a lousy job of keeping track of their feet.

Ritter turned around to admire his work. Fluid was seeping from the top of the Wanderer's hull, staining the cobblestones and letting off a putrid stench that reminded him of rotting fish.

That Wanderer was down for good; Ritter was sure of it. Might as well recover the rope and give Alger a rest before he found another one.

Ritter took down three more Wanderers before encountering a pair that had a crowd of people trapped on a bridge straddling the Seine. The alien machines had set their cages down and were casually cramming people into them like shoppers picking produce at a street market.

Ritter dismounted, leaving Alger a few hundred meters away from the enemy. He walked up to one of the cages, staying low and hoping the alien was too busy to notice him. This model was smaller than the cages he and the Marauders had found at the feeding ground north of Paris. It was also unlocked; the aliens must have been counting on fear and the fact that they usually carried the cages to keep their prey secure.

As soon as the alien placed a new victim inside and closed the door, Ritter ran around to the front with his pistol out and tore the door open. "Run!" he shouted, then bounced three rounds off the front of Wanderer's body before hurrying back to his horse.

The Wanderer hooted in rage and took off after him.

Ritter led the Wanderer away from the bridge and back down the way he'd come, stopping at a sturdy tree he'd spotted on the way. He had already tied the rope around the tree's thick trunk and draped the end over a branch, high enough that he wouldn't have to dismount to get it. This was closer to the operations the German Army had run during the first Martian invasion: games of cat and mouse that pulled the Wanderers into traps. But this game was much easier, thanks to Zimmerman's strategy of disabling the heat rays in advance.

He dug his heels into Alger and started his charge when a familiar sound reverberated in his gut: the hum of a heat ray.

No better time to remind himself to stay on task.

Ritter rode under the alien vehicle, looped one of its feet on the first try, and kept riding until Alger swerved to avoid a Panzer.

The cavalry had arrived, so to speak.

CHAPTER 38
PARIS, FRANCE

The countryside was different from inside a speeding automobile. The only sound was the whine of the complaining engine, and the only scents were warm leather and Benzin. The trees and fields were barely visible through the dirty windscreen at nearly thirty-five miles an hour. To Christian, it was such an awful way to travel. These infernal machines would probably disappear, forgotten, in a few years.

He had finally recognized the road south to Paris and been barreling down it for what seemed like hours when the outlines of the city finally appeared on the horizon. He pushed the car as fast as he dared. Were the Martians already on the attack?

He clutched the steering wheel so hard that his hands ached.

A horse-drawn cart popped into view. Hay bales hung over its sides, blocking the road and forcing Christian to come to a sliding stop. He honked the car's horn and inched the vehicle behind the cart as he aggressively revved the engine.

He noticed then that one of the gauges on the car's wood-paneled control cluster moved toward a red border. Was it for the water temperature? What did that mean?

Christian pounded the horn button on the steering wheel harder. Still no response from the horse-drawn cart.

Slowly they rolled down the road, the temperature gauge in the car's controls climbing higher and the minutes ticking away. Christian debated getting out of the car and trying to talk to the farmer when they reached a field and a wide spot in the road. He punched the accelerator and swerved to the side.

The automobile's stiff wheels were unforgiving when they met the stony field. Christian was nearly thrown from his seat, and he ran his tongue across his teeth to make sure he hadn't lost any as the farmer shook an indignant fist at him in the rearview mirror.

Christian clenched the wheel for the rest of the way. Finally, he was driving through the sixteenth arrondissement, and the Eiffel Tower came into view. He could stay on the right bank of the Seine and follow it around to headquarters.

He shifted the car back into high gear—and it stalled.

Verdammt!

Christian jumped out, grabbed the starting crank, and turned it. It flew out of his hands, forcing him to jump back to avoid losing a thumb. He'd forgotten the spark arrestor.

Scheiße!

He ran back to the cockpit to push it back and noticed the Benzin gauge. It read Empty.

Time to run, then. At least until Christian could find something faster.

He ran to the bridge that crossed the Seine by the Eiffel Tower and found himself moving against traffic. People were fleeing the city center in droves, and he had to push and shove to make his way across the river and past the tower. But his chances of finding a car or horse would be greater on the left bank.

He turned east, and soon he was running between the luxurious mansions and clubs of the seventh arrondissement. Finally, he spotted what the crowds had been fleeing: five or six hulking figures looming over the skyline, most seeming a kilometer or more away.

Christian's legs were lead weights by then, and his ribs burned. But he had to reach headquarters. He couldn't fight the aliens with only a single round.

He crossed into the sixth arrondissement, where he and Lage had been stranded before. Jardin du Luxembourg was ahead; he might find an abandoned car or horse there.

But Christian found chaos instead. Two Wanderers were herding people into the garden.

No time for that. He needed to get to headquarters or find some Marauders so that he could get more ammunition and a cart or Panzer.

But could he leave these people to their fates? How many would he save if he ran away while they were carted out of the city as the Martians' food?

Then he remembered the catacombs.

Of course. The Parisians were afraid of going to safety down there because of the Martians' Black Smoke during the first invasion. But the aliens weren't going to use the Smoke if they had come to harvest. And now Christian was standing less than a hundred meters from the stairs he'd taken into the catacombs with Lage.

He took off for the park at a full run. "The catacombs!" he shouted, thankful for Fluse's French lessons. "The catacombs! Come with me to the catacombs!"

"You fool!" a tall man with a bushy beard and huge arms bellowed back at him. "They'll only gas us!"

"No, they won't! They're hungry. They're collecting us for food. They won't use us if we're already dead!"

The tall man's eyes grew huge. "How do you know that?" he asked.

"The Marauders have been wiping out their harvesting machines. The Martians are desperate for food."

"Your accent . . . You're a Marauder."

"Yes, but that's not important right now. We need to lead

these people to the catacombs." Christian held out his hands as if pleading. "What have we got to lose?"

The man looked around, as if he hoped an answer would manifest before him. Finally, he nodded and started shouting for people to head to the stairs.

Christian turned to move into the crowd, but then a hand rested on his shoulder. "You've been in the catacombs?" the tall man asked him.

"Yes. Once."

"Then you know the path toward the old prison?"

"Yes, that's the way I took," Christian said and started to move again. "It should still be clear."

The man shook his head and held Christian by the shoulder. "Go start leading people down there," the tall man said, pointing in the direction of the entrance stairs.

"But—"

"You know the way, and you're a Marauder. That's two reasons why you need to get away from here alive."

The man spoke in a way that made it clear to Christian that he wasn't prepared to argue the point. But Christian knew the people of Paris would be more likely to believe a French person if one told them to go to the catacombs. But whether they followed Christian or not, they'd be safer once they were underground.

"Fine," Christian said, and took off for the stairs. His legs ached after the long run from the right bank of the Seine and across most of central Paris, but he pushed on.

A few people had already heeded the calls to head underground and were making the long trip down the 200-plus steps to the underground tunnels. Christian gently pushed, prodded, and pleaded for them to let him pass so he could guide them to safety. Some happily gave way; others argued, saying the Marauders were working with the Martians. But eventually, Christian made it down there.

A man was already checking and lighting torches when Christian stepped out into the clearing.

"Which way?" someone asked from behind Christian.

"West," he said.

The man lighting torches raised an eyebrow.

"If we take the tunnel west, it ends near the old military prison on rue de Cherche-Midi," Christian explained. "We can exit there, or wait until the Wanderers move on."

"You lead the way then," the man said. "I'll stay here and tell people where to go to find your group."

Christian picked up a torch and headed west, following the path the old veteran had taken him on during the riot. A small group, maybe a dozen people, followed right behind him.

"Are we really safe down here?" a woman asked after they'd gone a few hundred meters.

"You're safe," Christian said. "The Martians won't use their Smoke. They want to capture us alive."

"He's one of the Maraudeurs!" someone else whispered.

Christian pretended he didn't hear them.

The group proceeded slowly, and Christian sensed the crowd growing behind him as time ticked by. No reason to rush, though. They'd emerge from these tunnels less than a kilometer away. He established a relaxed pace, grateful for the chance to rest his tired legs.

When the group reached the gallery, the skulls taunted Christian in the flickering light of his torch. *What are you going to do now?* he swore he heard them ask. *Beat us with your empty rifle?*

Christian turned right and walked in the shadows of the arched part of the passageway. They were close. What would they find by the old prison?

"There's a well that way," he said, pointing toward the detour that led to the underground oasis.

"Do we have time?" a man asked.

"We're safe down here," Christian repeated. "We don't know what's aboveground. I'm getting a drink."

He strode down the side tunnel and eagerly scooped up the cool water, drinking in long, hungry gulps. Even after the slow walk through the cool tunnels, the well water was a welcome break, even though Christian's sore ribs made drinking painful.

Muffled complaints and the sounds of pushing and shoving interrupted his respite. A man had forced his way to the front of the group and was speaking in clipped, angry French that Christian had difficulty following.

"He wants to know when we'll be out of this tunnel," another man translated. It sounded like the man who'd spoken to Christian aboveground earlier, before they'd herded these people into the catacombs.

"Tell him we're about halfway, including the detour to this well," Christian said.

"He's very agitated. He wants to leave the tunnels now."

Christian shrugged. "We need to wait down here until the aliens are gone."

"Tell him to just go ahead and leave us alone!" someone else muttered.

No! Christian knew the tunnels were too shallow on the other end. The group couldn't risk attracting attention the Martians' attention.

"We can't leave the tunnels unless we know it's clear," Christian said. "If people run out and make too much noise, we'll all be in danger."

The translator repeated the message in French, and the group finally moved on.

Eventually, the tunnels started the familiar slope uphill. Soon, Christian and the others were at the bottom of a stairwell that was only six meters below street level.

"Wait here, and I'll see if it's clear," Christian said, holding up a hand to ensure the people understood.

He was on the second step when the sound of arguing voices, followed by the shuffling of a shoving match, alerted him that something was wrong. As he spun around to look, someone pushed him hard enough that he fell onto his face. Three people were bounding up the stairs. Before Christian could recover, two more ran in pursuit.

"No!" Christian shouted as they receded in the distance. "Stop!" He climbed the stairs after them as he shook his head to clear it.

An earsplitting blast from a Wanderer, followed by human screams, stopped him in his tracks. They'd run right into an alien.

Christian turned and bounded back down the stairs. He needed to get the people back into the deeper part of the tunnels without causing a panic, but it was already too late. The tunnels had erupted into chaos.

Before he reached the crowd, a pair of tentacles snaked down the stairs. He pressed himself against the wall as they passed. They grabbed two people and pulled them back to the surface.

Mein Gott. Christian hadn't led these people through these tunnels so he could serve them up two at a time.

He charged up the stairs, screaming at the top of his lungs. If he had to join the people in the cage to save them, he would.

He hit the street at a full run, bellowing and waving his arms. "Me! Me! Take me, you alien bastards!"

He danced back and forth in front of the Wanderer. The alien vehicle paused for a moment, as if considering him.

Then Christian froze as he heard the throbbing buzz of a heat ray.

The Wanderer tipped forward, forcing him to turn and run as it fell to the ground with a crash of rending metal. He spun back to face the fallen Wanderer and found a Panzer instead.

The Marauders had arrived. The people were safe.

Christian's knees went out from under him. He dropped to the ground.

"Christian!" It was Fluse, shouting as he exited the Panzer and ran toward him. "Are you hurt?"

"I'm fine." Christian pointed to the entrance where the

Wanderer's inert tentacles led. "People . . . catacombs . . . over there."

The crowd was already emerging from underground. Some were laughing. Others cried in obvious relief when they saw the downed Wanderer and the Panzer.

"What's going on?" Fluse asked as he helped Christian to his feet. "You led them here?"

Christian explained what had happened since he'd left headquarters. As he finished, a woman clutching a young girl's hand approached them.

"Que Dieu vous bénisse," the woman said with tears in her eyes.

"You saved them," Fluse said. "We might not have gotten there soon enough to keep the Martians from taking them away. They were here trying to restock for a new feeding area we found down south."

Christian had saved them. Without firing a single shot.

CHAPTER 39

GOUSSAINVILLE, FRANCE

Christian let out a long sigh of relief as he climbed off his horse. His ribs were still sore, but the ride had been worth it. It had been a long three days since his aborted first try, but he'd finally made it to Goussainville. Fortunately, the village had been untouched by the recent violence.

"We made it," Lage said with a broad grin.

"Yes, we did," Christian replied.

"Oh yes, I'm so relieved," Ritter said as he rolled his eyes. "I was on the edge of my saddle, worrying about your girlfriend the whole way."

Christian opened his mouth to respond, then caught himself. There was nothing to be gained by encouraging Ritter.

Not a single Wanderer had been seen since their failed attack on Paris. Had they spent all their forces in that last, desperate effort? Or had their failure forced them into hiding? Only time would tell, Christian guessed. Either way, Paris now had a chance to recover and rebuild.

So did Germany. They'd applied the Marauders' strategy to the Martian feeding grounds over there and fared even better since the disastrous attack on Berlin. For the first time in many months, Central and Western Europe felt safe.

Even though the fall harvest had been meager, Goussainville was bustling. A group of children were playing by the well. Louis was busy arranging the first squashes of the year, while the bakery had enough pies that they were selling them from a table in front of the shop.

"I'm going over there and getting myself an entire pie," Lage said.

"Good idea," Ritter said. "And I will see what they have for my trip east."

"You already have two sandwiches and a half dozen apples," Lage said.

"Don't question your betters, boy."

Christian absentmindedly rubbed his sore side as Lage and Ritter walked away. He should have sent word ahead, or at least tried to learn where Charlotte had ended up staying. How would he find her? Did she even want to be found?

He leaned on the cart and scanned the town square. A group of six or seven children chased each other in circles by the well. Most of the girls looked to be about nine or ten years old, about the same age as Patty.

Christian strode toward them for a closer look. Patty was there, gleefully playing with the other children.

Tension that Christian hadn't known he was carrying melted away. Patty was safe; and instead of playing war, she was playing tag with children her age.

Almost as if she read his mind, Patty turned and looked at him. "Christian!" she exclaimed as she broke away from the group and ran over to give him a surprisingly powerful hug.

"Hi Patty," Christian said in French. He wrapped an arm around her and suppressed the urge to complain about his ribs.

"Mommy said Paris is safe now."

"Yes. It is."

"So now you can stay here with us."

Christian flushed. He wanted that more than anything else in the world. But did Charlotte feel the same way? Or had he wasted his time coming here?

"It's you," said a voice from behind Christian.

He turned and faced a woman with a vaguely familiar face. Where had he seen her before?

"You fixed the wheel on our cart and sent us here," she said.

Yes. She'd hidden behind her cart with her daughter as Christian and Emil had repaired it on their way to Ritter's camp. In between what they'd found and what had happened since then, Christian had forgotten about that afternoon.

"That's right," Christian said. "We sent you here. I'm glad you made it safely."

"Only because of you and your friend," the woman said with a smile. "Thank you."

Christian smiled nervously, then turned back to Patty, who had finally released her grip on his sore midsection. "Do you know where your mother is?" he asked.

"At the church with the monseigneur," Patty answered. "I'm going to start school there!" Then she ran away to continue playing with her friends. One of them was the little girl who had hidden behind the cart on the road.

Christian turned and looked across the square, searching for Charlotte.

There she was, standing near the église, talking to the monseigneur. When had he ridden up here?

Christian took a deep breath and started toward them.

"Herr Beckenbauer! Christian!" It was Louis, running from behind his stand. "You're here! I was hoping we'd see you. We've all heard what you and the Marauders did for Paris! I was hoping we'd have a chance to thank you."

Christian smiled and nodded nervously. Why did their thanks make him feel so uncomfortable?

Charlotte had turned at the sound of Louis's voice, and now she looked directly at Christian. She tilted her head and raised an eyebrow.

Christian smiled and waved. "Thank you, Louis," he said, keeping his gaze on Charlotte.

She broke into a tremendous smile and blushed.

"No, no, you saved more than a hundred lives," Louis exclaimed. "You deserve the thanks, not me!"

"Of course, Louis," Christian said, his eyes still locked on Charlotte. "Thank you."

"Will you be staying here long?" Louis asked. "Can I get you something for the ride back to Paris?"

"Um, yes Louis. Whatever you say," Christian said, and he finally walked over to the église.

"Christian!" the monseigneur said as Christian reached him and Charlotte. "It's nice to see you here."

He extended a hand. Christian looked at it for a moment, then took it and returned the handshake.

"We were just talking about you," Charlotte said, still wearing her smile. "I hope you're feeling better."

"I am now," Christian said.

"Well, I need to get set up for confession," the monseigneur said. "We can finish talking about getting Patricia set up in school when it reopens, Charlotte. We're almost finished recovering from that attack by the ravageur car, and we'd love to have her."

"Yes, Monseigneur," Charlotte said. "Thank you."

The monseigneur turned and entered the church.

"You came," Charlotte said, turning back to Christian.

"I said I would," Christian said.

Charlotte's smile brightened. "Yes, you did."

"I saw Patty already. How is your father?"

"Doing well. Louis arranged for a place for us to stay. It has a garden, and we may be able to work some of the land up here. Patty has made friends already and will start school next week. I'm glad you sent us here. I hadn't realized how important it was to get Patty around children her age."

"She does seem very happy over there," Christian said with a nod.

"I hid her soldiers and threw away that horrible toy Wanderer last week. She hasn't noticed yet."

Christian let out a sigh of relief.

Charlotte hesitated before saying, "Are you really—"

"So, you found her?" Ritter said, aiming his last comment at Charlotte. He was sitting atop his horse with an apple in one hand. "He talked about you for the whole ride up here, you know."

Christian's heart jumped into his throat. "I did not!" he said. What was Ritter trying to do?

"You didn't?" Charlotte said with a sniffle. "I thought you cared."

Christian's mouth gaped, and Charlotte laughed out loud at his response.

"I'm glad to see there's someone up here to keep you out of trouble," Ritter said. "Well, I'm off now. Look for me in Berlin if you tire of the good life. Your friend Schmidt will be meeting me out there as soon as he's off those crutches."

He waved and rode off before Christian could answer.

"Who was that?" Charlotte asked with a mischievous grin. "I like him."

Christian wiped a bead of sweat from his brow.

"Wait." Charlotte touched Christian's shoulder. "Did I embarrass you?"

"I . . . uh . . . you were going to ask me something before you were interrupted."

"Oh yes. I was going to ask you if you're really finished."

"Yes," Christian said, without a moment's hesitation. "Yes, I am."

Charlotte looked him in the eye for nearly a minute, then took his hand.

The children's game of tag was still in progress. Patty was pursuing an older boy around the town square. He leaped up on the edge of the well just as he was about to tap him on the back, and she followed with a tremendous jump. She overshot and teetered on the edge.

Christian broke away from Charlotte and caught Patty around the waist. "I've got you," he said.

———

THE GREAT WAR OF THE WORLDS WILL CONTINUE IN OCTOBER 2025!

If you read *Shadows in the Past*, you might be wondering what's happening in the United States right now. (If you haven't read it, *what are you waiting for???*)

Murder in Soft Words will answer all your questions in October 2025! You'll learn what James is up to, why Susan isn't very happy with him, and what happened to Fleming!

Pre-order *Murder in Soft Words* today so you get it the day it's published!

ABOUT THE AUTHOR

I'm Eric Goebelbecker. I write stuff.

I'm the author of *Shadows of the Past* and *Clouds in the Future* the first two books in an ongoing series about the aftermath of the Martin invasion in the War of the Worlds. The next book, *Murder in Soft Words,* is available for pre-order and will arrive in October 2025.

I was lucky enough to inherit an incurable curiosity about technology and a tremendous love of science fiction from his father. Both led to a career repairing radars in the U.S. Army, followed by another as a programmer on Wall Street. Now, I write about technology and train dogs, as well as work on my sci-fi and fantasy stories.

If you're not already a subscriber, you can find my email list here, get a free short story about Ben Johnson and James Brogan's father, and get the latest news on my next book and short stories.

Find me at my newsletter, on my website, and on the social links below.

And please consider leaving a review!

facebook.com/egoebelbecker

instagram.com/egoebelbecker

bsky.app/profile/ericgoebelbecker.com